"Here's an Easter greeting that snarls . . . opens a surprise Pandora's box . . . the ending is an unexpected shocker. Mr. Blish has a capricious, deadly sense of humor. One you'll remember."

Kirkus Service

"James Blish is one of the most powerful writers to come down the pike in some time. And he is going to scare you."

State Journal Register
(Springfield, Mass.)

"Blish combines a contemporary setting, black magic and suspense to produce a novel which is very difficult to put down and makes its point in a terrifying resolution."

Standard Times (Mass.)

This novel completes a trilogy with the overall title of *After Such Knowledge*. The previous volumes (which are independent of each other except for subject matter) are *Doctor Mirabilis* and *A Case of Conscience*.

JAMES BLISH

BLACK EASTER

or
Faust Aleph-Null

Why, this is Hell; nor am I out of it.
CHRISTOPHER MARLOWE

A DELL BOOK

In Memoriam
C. S. LEWIS

Published by
DELL PUBLISHING CO., INC.
750 Third Avenue
New York, N.Y. 10017
Copyright © 1968 by James Blish
All rights reserved
Dell ® TM 681510, Dell Publishing Co., Inc.
Reprinted by arrangement with
Doubleday and Company, Inc.
Garden City, N.Y.
Printed in the U.S.A.
First Dell printing—July 1969

A short version of this novel was published
under the title *Faust Aleph-Null,*
copyright © 1967 by Galaxy Publishing Corporation.

Text figures by Judith Ann Lawrence

AUTHOR'S NOTE

There have been many novels, poems and plays about magic and witchcraft. All of them that I have read—which I think includes the vast majority—classify without exception as either romantic or playful, Thomas Mann's included. I have never seen one which dealt with what real sorcery actually had to be like if it existed, although all the grimoires are explicit about the matter. Whatever other merits this book may have, it neither romanticizes magic nor treats it as a game.

Technically, its background is based as closely as possible upon the writings and actual working manuals of practicing magicians working in the Christian tradition from the thirteenth to the eighteenth centuries, from the *Ars Magna* of Ramon Lull, through the various *Keys* of pseudo-Solomon, pseudo-Agrippa, pseudo-Honorius and so on, to the grimoires themselves. All of the books mentioned in the text actually exist; there are no "Necronomicons" or other such invented works, and the quotations and symbols are equally authentic. (Though of course it should be added that the attributions of these works are seldom to be trusted; as C. A. E. Waite has noted, the besetting *bibliographic* sins of magic are imputed authorship, false places of publication and backdating.)

For most readers this will be warning enough. The experimentally minded, however, should be further warned that, although the quotations, diagrams and rituals in the novel are authentic, they are in no case complete. The book is not, and was not intended to be, either synoptic or encyclopedic. It is not a *vade mecum*, but a *cursus infamam*.

James Blish

Alexandria (Va.), 1968

STATIONS

PREPARATION
OF THE
OPERATOR

It is not reasonable to suppose that Aristotle knew the number of the Elect.

—Albertus Magnus

The room stank of demons.

And it was not just the room—which would have been unusual, but not unprecedented. Demons were not welcome visitors on Monte Albano, where the magic practiced was mostly of the kind called Transcendental, aimed at pursuit of a more perfect mystical union with God and His two revelations, the Scriptures and the World. But occasionally, Ceremonial magic—an applied rather than a pure art, seeking certain immediate advantages—was practiced also, and in the course of that the White Monks sometimes called down a demiurge, and, even more rarely, raised up one of the Fallen.

That had not happened in a long time, however; of that, Father F. X. Domenico Bruno Garelli was now positive. No, the stench was something in the general air. It was, in fact, something that was abroad in the world . . . the secular world, God's world, the world at large.

And it would have to be something extraordinarily powerful, extraordinarily malign, for Father Domenico to have detected it without prayer, without ritual, without divination, without instruments or instrumentalities of any kind. Though Father Domenico—ostensibly an ordinary Italian monk of about forty *ae,* with the stolid face of his peasant family and calluses on his feet—was in fact an adept of the highest class, the class called Karcists, he was not a Sensitive. There were no true Sensitives at all on the mountain, for they did not thrive even in the relative isolation of a monastery; they could not function except as eremites (which explained why there were so few of them anywhere in the world, these days).

Father Domenico closed the huge Book of Hours with a creak of leather and parchment, and rolled up the palimpsest upon which he had been calculating. There was no doubt about it: none of the White Monks had invoked any infernal power, not even a minor seneschal, for more than a twelve-month past. He had suspected as much—how, after all, could he have gone unaware of such an event?—but the records, which kept themselves without possibility of human intervention, confirmed it. That exhalation from Hellmouth was drifting up from the world below.

Deeply disturbed, Father Domenico rested his elbows upon the closed record book and propped his chin in his hands. The question was, what should he do now? Tell Father Umberto? No, he really had too little solid information yet to convey to anyone else, let alone disturbing the Director-General with his suspicions and groundless certainties.

How, then, to find out more? He looked ruefully to his right, at his crystal. He had never been able to make it work—probably because he knew all too well that what Roger Bacon had really been describing in *The Nullity of Magic* had been nothing more than a forerunner of the telescope—though others on the mountain, unencumbered by such historical skepticism, practiced crystallomancy with considerable success. To his left, next to the book, a small brass telescope was held aloft in a regrettably phallic position by a beautiful gold statuette of Pan that had a golden globe for a pediment, but which was only a trophy of an old triumph over a minor Piedmontese black magician and had no astronomical usefulness; should Father Domenico want to know the precise positions of the lesser Jovian satellites (the Galilean ones were of course listed in the U. S. Naval Observatory ephemeris), or anything else necessary to the casting of an absolute horoscope, he would call upon the twelve-inch telescope and the image-orthicon on the roof of the monastery and have the images (should he need them as well as the data) transmitted by closed-circuit television directly to his room. At the moment, unhappily, he had no event to cast a horoscope either from or toward—only a pervasive, immensurable fog of rising evil.

At Father Domenico's back, he knew without looking, colored spots and lozenges of light from his high, narrow, stained-glass window were being cast at this hour across the face of his computer, mocking the little colored points of its safe-lights. He was in charge of this machine, which the other Brothers regarded with an awe he privately thought perilously close to being superstitious; he himself knew the computer to be nothing but a moron—an idiot-savant with a gift for fast addition. But he had no data to feed the machine, either.

Call for a Power and ask for help? No, not yet. The occasion might be trivial, or at least seem so in the spheres they moved, and where they moved. Father Domenico gravely doubted that it was, but he had been rebuked before for unnecessarily troubling those movers and governors, and it was not a kind of displeasure a sensible white magician could afford, however in contempt he might hold the indiscriminate hatred of demons.

No; there was no present solution but to write to Father Uccello, who would listen hungrily, if nothing else. He was a Sensitive; he, too, would know that something ugly was being born—and would doubtless know more about it than that. He would have data.

Father Domenico realized promptly that he had been almost unconsciously trying to avoid this decision almost from the start. The reason was obvious, now that he looked squarely at it; for of all the possibilities, this one would be the most time-consuming. But it also seemed to be unavoidable.

Resignedly, he got out his Biro fountain pen and a sheet of foolscap and began. What few facts he had could be briefly set down, but there was a certain amount of ceremony that had to be observed: salutations in Christ, inquiries about health, prayers and so on, and of course the news; Sensitives were always as lonely as old women, and as interested in gossip about sin, sickness and death. One had to placate them; edifying them—let alone curing them—was impossible.

While he was still at it, the door swung inward to admit an acolyte: the one Father Domenico, in a rare burst of sportiveness, had nicknamed Joannes, after Bacon's famous disappearing apprentice. Looking up at him bemusedly, Father Domenico said:

"I'm not through yet."

"I beg your pardon?"

"Sorry . . . I was thinking about something else. I'll have a letter for you to send down the mountain in a while. In the meantime, what did you want?"

"Myself, nothing," Joannes said. "But the Director asks me to tell you that he wishes your presence, in the office, right after sext. There's to be a meeting with a client."

"Oh. Very well. What sort of client?"

"I don't know, Father. It's a new one. He's being hauled up the mountain now. I hear he's a rich American, but then, a lot of them are, aren't they?"

"You do seem to know *something*," Father Domenico said drily, but his mind was not on the words. The reek of evil had suddenly become much more pronounced; it was astonishing that the boy couldn't smell it too. He put the letter aside. By tonight there would be more news to add—and, perhaps, data. "Tell the Director I'll be along promptly."

"First I have to go and tell Father Amparo," Joannes said. "He's supposed to meet the client too."

Father Domenico nodded. At the door, the acolyte turned, with a mysterious sort of slyness, and added:

"His name is Baines."

The door shut. Well, there was a fact, such as it was —and obviously Joannes had thought it full of significance. But to Father Domenico it meant nothing at all.

Nothing, nothing at all.

THE FIRST COMMISSION

[In] the legendary wonder-world of Theurgy . . . all paradoxes seem to obtain actually, contradictions co-exist logically, the effect is greater than the cause and the shadow more than the substance. Therein the visible melts into the unseen, the invisible is manifested openly, motion from place to place is accomplished without traversing the intervening distance, matter passes through matter. . . . There life is prolonged, youth renewed, physical immortality secured. There earth becomes gold, and gold earth. There words and wishes possess creative power, thoughts are things, desire realizes its object. There, also, the dead live and the hierarchies of extra-mundane intelligence are within easy communication, and become ministers or tormentors, guides or destroyers, of man.

—A. E. Waite, *The Book of Ceremonial Magic*

I

The magician said, "No, I can't help you to persuade a woman. Should you want her raped, I can arrange that. If you want to rape her yourself, I can arrange that, too, with more difficulty—possibly more than you'd have to exert on your own hook. But I can't supply you with any philtres or formulae. My specialty is crimes of violence. Chiefly, murder."

Baines shot a sidelong glance at his special assistant, Jack Ginsberg, who as usual wore no expression whatsoever and had not a crease out of true. It was nice to be able to trust someone. Baines said, "You're very frank."

"I try to leave as little mystery as possible," Theron Ware—Baines knew that was indeed his real name—said promptly. "From the client's point of view, black magic is a body of technique, like engineering. The more he knows about it, the easier I find it makes coming to an agreement."

"No trade secrets? Arcane lore, and so on?"

"Some—mostly the products of my own research, and very few of them of any real importance to you. The main scholium of magic is 'arcane' only because most people don't know what books to read or where to find them. Given those books—and sometimes, somebody to translate them for you—you could learn almost everything important that I know in a year. To make something of the material, of course, you'd have to have the talent, since magic is also an art. With books and the gift, you could become a magician—either you are or you aren't, there are no bad magicians, any more than there is such a thing as a bad mathematician—in about twenty years. If it didn't kill you first, of course, in some equivalent of a laboratory accident. It takes that long, give or take a few years, to develop the skills involved. I don't mean to say you wouldn't find it formidable, but the age of secrecy is past. And really the old codes were rather simple-minded, much easier to read than, say, musical notation. If they weren't, well, computers could break them in a hurry."

Most of these generalities were familiar stuff to Baines, as Ware doubtless knew. Baines suspected the magician of offering them in order to allow time for himself to be studied by the client. This suspicion crystallized promptly as a swinging door behind Ware's huge desk chair opened silently, and a short-skirted blond girl in a pageboy coiffure came in with a letter on a small silver tray.

"Thank you, Greta. Excuse me," Ware said, taking the tray. "We wouldn't have been interrupted if this weren't important." The envelope cracked expensively in his hands as he opened it.

Baines watch the girl go out—a moving object, to be sure, but except that she reminded him vaguely of someone else, nothing at all extraordinary—and then went openly about inspecting Ware. As usual, he started with the man's chosen surroundings.

The magician's office, brilliant in the afternoon sunlight, might have been the book-lined study of any doctor or lawyer, except that the room and the furniture were outsize. That said very little about Ware, for the house was a rented cliffside palazzo; there were

bigger ones available in Positano had Ware been interested in still higher ceilings and worse acoustics.
Though most of the books looked old, the office was
no mustier than, say, the library of Merton College,
and it contained far fewer positively ancient instruments. The only trace in it that might have been
attributable to magic was a faint smell of mixed in-
censes, which the Tyrrhenian air coming in through
the opened windows could not entirely dispel; but it
was so slight that the nose soon tired of trying to
detect it. Besides, it was hardly diagnostic by itself;
small Italian churches, for instance, also smelled like
that—and so did the drawing rooms of Egyptian police
chiefs.

Ware himself was remarkable, but with only a single
exception, only in the sense that all men are unique
to the eye of the born captain. A small, spare man he
was, dressed in natural Irish tweeds, a French-cuffed
shirt linked with what looked like ordinary steel, a
narrow, gray, silk four-in-hand tie with a single very
small sapphire chessman—a rook—tacked to it. His
leanness seemed to be held together with cables;
Baines was sure that he was physically strong, despite
a marked pallor, and that his belt size had not changed
since he had been in high school.

His present apparent age was deceptive. His face
was seamed, and his bushy gray eyebrows now only
slightly suggested that he had once been red-haired.
His hair proper could not, for—herein lay his one
marked oddity—he was tonsured, like a monk, blue
veins crawling across his bare white scalp as across the
papery backs of his hands. An innocent bystander
might have taken him to be in his late sixties. Baines
knew him to be exactly his own age, which was forty-
eight. Black magic, not surprisingly, was obviously a
wearing profession; cerebrotonic types like Ware, as

Baines had often observed of the scientists who worked for Consolidated Warfare Service (div. A. O. LeFebre et Cie.), ordinarily look about forty-five from a real age of thirty until their hair turns white, if a heart attack doesn't knock them off in the interim.

The parchment crackled and Jack Ginsberg unobtrusively touched his dispatch case, setting going again a tape recorder back in Rome. Baines thought Ware saw this, but chose to take no notice. The magician said:

"Of course, it's also faster if my clients are equally frank with me."

"I should think you'd know all about me by now," Baines said. He felt an inner admiration. The ability to pick up an interrupted conversation exactly where it had been left off is rare in a man. Women do it easily, but seldom to any purpose.

"Oh, Dun and Bradstreet," Ware said, "newspaper morgues, and of course the grapevine—I have all that, naturally. But I'll still need to ask some questions."

"Why not read my mind?"

"Because it's more work than it's worth. I mean your excellent mind no disrespect, Mr. Baines. But one thing you must understand is that magic is hard work. I don't use it out of laziness, I am not a lazy man, but by the same token I do take the easier ways of getting what I want if easier ways are available."

"You've lost me."

"An example, then. All magic—I repeat, *all* magic, with no exceptions whatsoever—depends upon the control of demons. By demons I mean specifically fallen angels. No lesser class can do a thing for you. Now, I know one such whose earthly form includes a long tongue. You may find the notion comic."

"Not exactly."

"Let that pass for now. In any event, this is also a great prince and president, whose apparition would cost me three days of work and two weeks of subsequent exhaustion. Shall I call him up to lick stamps for me?"

"I see the point," Baines said. "All right, ask your questions."

"Thank you. Who sent you to me?"

"A medium in Bel Air—Los Angeles. She attempted to blackmail me, so nearly successfully that I concluded that she did have some real talent and would know somebody who had more. I threatened her life and she broke."

Ware was taking notes. "I see. And she sent you to the Rosicrucians?"

"She tried, but I already knew that dodge. She sent me to Monte Albano."

"Ah. That surprises me, a little. I wouldn't have thought that you'd have any need of treasure finders."

"I do and I don't," Baines said. "I'll explain that, too, but a little later, if you don't mind. Primarily I wanted someone in your specialty—murder—and of course the white monks were of no use there. I didn't even broach the subject with them. Frankly, I only wanted to test your reputation, of which I'd had hints. I, too, can use newspaper morgues. Their horror when I mentioned you was enough to convince me that I ought to talk to you, at least."

"Sensible. Then you don't really believe in magic yet—only in ESP or some such nonsense."

"I'm not," Baines said guardedly, "a religious man."

"Precisely put. Hence, you want a demonstration. Did you bring with you the mirror I mentioned on the phone to your assistant?"

Silently, Jack took from his inside jacket pocket a

waxed-paper envelope, from which he in turn removed a lady's hand mirror sealed in glassine. He handed it to Baines, who broke the seal.

"Good. Look in it."

Out of the corners of Baines' eyes, two slow thick tears of dark venous blood were crawling down beside his nose. He lowered the mirror and stared at Ware.

"Hypnotism," he said, quite steadily. "I had hoped for better."

"Wipe them off," Ware said, unruffled.

Baines pulled out his immaculate monogrammed handkerchief. On the white-on-white fabric, the red stains turned slowly into butter-yellow gold.

"I suggest you take those to a government metallurgist tomorrow," Ware said. "I could hardly have hypnotized him. Now perhaps we might get down to business."

"I thought you said—"

"That even the simplest trick requires a demon. So I did, and I meant it. He is sitting at your back now, Mr. Baines, and he will be there until day after tomorrow at this hour. Remember that—day after tomorrow. It will cost me dearly to have turned this little piece of silliness, but I'm used to having to do such things for a skeptical client—and it will be included in my bill. Now, if you please, Mr. Baines, what *do* you want?"

Baines handed the handkerchief to Jack, who folded it carefully and put it back in its waxed-paper wrapper. "I," Baines said, "of course want somebody killed. Tracelessly."

"Of course, but who?"

"I'll tell you that in a minute. First of all, do you exercise any scruples?"

"Quite a few," Ware said. "For instance, I don't

kill my friends, not for any client. And possibly I might balk at certain strangers. However, in general, I do have strangers sent for, on a regular scale of charges."

"Then we had better explore the possibilities," Baines said. "I've got an ex-wife who's a gross inconvenience to me. Do you balk at that?"

"Has she any children—by you or anybody else?"

"No, none at all."

"In that case, there's no problem. For that kind of job, my standard fee is fifteen thousand dollars, flat."

Despite himself, Baines stared in astonishment. "Is that all?" he said at last.

"That's all. I suspect that I'm almost as wealthy as you are, Mr. Baines. After all, I can find treasure as handily as the white monks can—indeed, a good deal better. I use these alimony cases to keep my name before the public. Financially they're a loss to me."

"What kinds of fees are you interested in?"

"I begin to exert myself slightly at about five million."

If this man was a charlatan, he was a grandiose one. Baines said, "Let's stick to the alimony case for the moment. Or rather, suppose I don't care about the alimony, as in fact I don't. Instead, I might not only want her dead, but I might want her to die badly. To suffer."

"I don't charge extra for that."

"Why not?"

"Mr. Baines," Ware said patiently, "I remind you, please, that I myself am not a killer. I merely summon and direct the agent. I think it very likely—in fact, I think it beyond doubt—that any patient I have sent for dies in an access of horror and agony beyond your power to imagine, or even of mine. But you did specify that you wanted your murder done 'tracelessly,' which obviously means that I must have no unusual marks left on the patient. I prefer it that way myself. How then could I prove suffering if you asked for it, in a way inarguable enough to charge you extra for it?"

"Or, look at the other side of the shield, Mr. Baines. Every now and then, an unusual divorce client asks that the exconsort be carried away painlessly, even sweetly, out of some residue of sentiment. I *could* collect an extra fee for that, on a contingent basis, that is, if the body turns out to show no overt marks of disease or violence. But my agents are demons, and sweetness is not a trait they can be compelled to exhibit, so I never accept that kind of condition from a client, either. Death is what you pay for, and death is what you get. The circumstances are up to the agent, and I don't offer my clients anything that I know I can't deliver."

"All right, I'm answered," Baines said. "Forget Dolores—actually she's only a minor nuisance, and only one of several, for that matter. Now let's talk about the other end of the spectrum. Suppose instead that I should ask you to . . . send for . . . a great political figure. Say, the governor of California—or, if he's a friend of yours, pick a similar figure who isn't."

Ware nodded. "He'll do well enough. But you'll recall that I asked you about children. Had you really turned out to have been an alimony case, I should next have asked you about surviving relatives. My fees rise in direct proportion to the numbers and kinds of people a given death is likely to affect. This is partly what you call scruples, and partly a species of self-defense. Now in the case of a reigning governor, I would charge you one dollar for every vote he got when he was last elected. Plus expenses, of course."

Baines whistled in admiration. "You're the first man I've ever met who's worked out a system to make scruples pay. And I can see why you don't care about alimony cases. Someday, Mr. Ware—"

"*Doctor* Ware, please. I am a Doctor of Theology."

"Sorry. I only meant to say that someday I'll ask you why you want so much money. You aesthetics seldom can think of any good use for it. In the meantime, however, you're hired. Is it all payable in advance?"

"The expenses are payable in advance. The fee is C.O.D. As you'll realize once you stop to think about it, Mr. Baines—"

"*Doctor* Baines. I am an LL.D."

"Apologies in exchange. I want you to realize, after these courtesies, that I have never, never been bilked."

Baines thought about what was supposed to be at his back until day after tomorrow. Pending the test of the golden tears on the handkerchief, he was willing to believe that he should not try to cheat Ware. Actually, he had never planned to.

"Good," he said, getting up. "By the same token, we don't need a contract. I agree to your terms."

"But what for?"

"Oh," Baines said. "we can use the governor of California for a starter. Jack here will iron out any remaining details with you. I have to get back to Rome by tonight."

"You did say, 'For a starter?' "

Baines nodded shortly. Ware, also rising, said, "Very well. I shall ask no questions. But in fairness, Mr. Baines, I should warn you that on your next commission of this kind, I shall ask you what *you* want."

"By that time," Baines said, holding his excitement tightly bottled, "we'll *have* to exchange such confidences. Oh, Dr. Ware, will the, uh, demon on my back go away by itself when the time's up, or must I see you again to get it taken off?"

"It isn't *on* your back," Ware said. "And it will go by itself. Marlowe to the contrary, misery does not love company."

Baring his teeth, Baines said, "We'll see about that."

II

For a moment, Jack Ginsberg felt the same soon-to-be-brief strangeness of the man who does not really know what is going on and hence thinks he might be about to be fired. It was as though something had swallowed him by mistake, and—quite without malice—was about to throw him up again.

While he waited for the monster's nausea to settle out, Jack went through his rituals, stroking his cheeks for stubble, resettling his creases, running through last week's accounts, and thinking above all, as he usually did most of all in such interims, of what the new girl might look like squatting in her stockings. Nothing special, probably; the reality was almost always hedged around with fleshly inconveniences and piddling little preferences that he could flense away at will from the clean vision.

When the chief had left and Ware had come back to his desk, however, Jack was ready for business and thoroughly on top of it. He prided himself upon an absolute self-control.

"Questions?" Ware said, leaning back easily.

"A few, Dr. Ware. You mentioned expenses. What expenses?"

"Chiefly travel," Ware said. "I have to see the patient, personally. In the case Dr. Baines posed, that involves a trip to California, which is a vast inconvenience to me, and goes on the bill. It includes air fare, hotels, meals, other out-of-pocket expenses, which I'll itemize when the mission is over. Then there's the question of getting to see the governor. I have colleagues in California, but there's a certain amount of influence I'll have to buy, even with the help of Consolidated Warfare—munitions and magic are circles that don't inersect very effectively. On the whole, I think a draft for ten thousand would be none too small."

All that for magic. Disgusting. But the chief believed in it, at least provisionally. It made Jack feel very queasy.

"That sounds satisfactory," he said, but he made no move toward the corporate checkbook; he was not about to issue any Valentines to strangers yet, not until there was more love touring about the landscape than he had felt in his crew-cut antennae. "We're naturally a little bit wondering, sir, why all this expense is necessary. We understand that you'd rather not ride a demon when you can fly a jet with less effort—"

"I'm not sure you do," Ware said, "but stop simpering about it and ask me about the money."

"Argh . . . well, sir, then, just why do you live outside the United States? We know you're still a citizen. And after all, we have freedom of religion in the States still. Why does the chief have to pay to ship you back home for one job?"

"Because I'm not a common gunman," Ware said. "Because I don't care to pay income taxes, or even report my income to anybody. There are two reasons. For the benefit of your ever-attentive dispatch case there—since you're a deaf ear if ever I saw one—if I lived in the United States and advertised myself as a magician, I would be charged with fraud, and if I successfully defended myself—proved I was what I said I was—I'd wind up in a gas chamber. If I failed to defend myself, I'd be just one more charlatan. In Europe, I can say I'm a magician, and be left alone if I can satisfy my clients—*caveat emptor*. Otherwise, I'd have to be constantly killing off petty politicians and accountants, which isn't worth the work, and sooner or later runs into the law of diminishing returns. Now you can turn that thing off."

Aha; there *was* something wrong with this joker. He was preying upon superstition. As a Reformed Orthodox Agnostic, Jack Ginsberg knew all the ins and outs of that, especially the double-entry sides. He said smoothly:

"I quite understand. But don't you perhaps have almost as much trouble with the Church, here in Italy, as you would with the government back home?"

"No, not under a liberal pontificate. The modern Church discourages what it calls superstition among its adherents. I haven't encountered a prelate in decades who believes in the *literal* existence of demons— though of course some of the Orders know better."

"To be sure," Jack said, springing his trap exultantly. "So I think, sir, that you may be overcharging us—and haven't been quite candid with us. If you do indeed control all these great princes and presidents, you could as easily bring the chief a woman as you could bring him a treasure or a murder."

"So I could," the magician said, a little wearily. "I see you've done a little reading. But I explained to Dr. Baines, and I explain again to you, that I specialize only in crimes of violence. Now, Mr. Ginsberg, I think you were about to write me an expense check."

"So I was." But still he hesitated. At last Ware said with delicate politeness:

"Is there some other doubt I could resolve for you, Mr. Ginsberg? I am, after all, a Doctor of Theology.

Or perhaps you have a private commission you wish to broach to me?"

"No," Jack said. "No, not exactly."

"I see no reason why you should be shy. It's clear that you like my lamia. And in fact, she's quite free of the nuisances of human women that so annoy you—"

"Damn you. I *thought* you read minds! You lied about that, too."

"I don't read minds, and I never lie," Ware said. "But I'm adept at reading faces and somatotypes. It saves me a lot of trouble, and a lot of unnecessary magic. Do you want the creature or don't you? I could have her sent to you invisibly if you like."

"No."

"Not invisibly. I'm sorry for you. Well then, my godless and lustless friend, speak up for yourself. What *would* you like? Your business is long since done. Spit it out. What is it?"

For a breathless instant, Jack almost said what it was, but the God in which he no longer believed was at his back. He made out the check and handed it over. The girl (no, not a girl) came in and took it away.

"Good-bye," Theron Ware said.

He had missed the boat again.

III

Father Domenico read the letter again, hopefully. Father Uccello affected an Augustinian style, after his name saint, full of rare words and outright neologisms imbedded in medieval syntax—as a stylist, Father Domenico much preferred Roger Bacon, but that eminent anti-magician, not being a Father of the Church, tempted few imitators—and it was possible that Father Domenico had misread him. But no; involuted though the Latin of the letter was, the sense, this time, was all too plain.

Father Domenico sighed. The practice of Ceremonial magic, at least of the white kind which was the monastery's sole concern, seemed to be becoming increasingly unrewarding. Part of the difficulty, of course, lay in the fact that the chiefest traditional use (for profit) of white magic was the finding of buried treasure; and after centuries of unremitting practice by centuries of sorcerers black and white, plus the irruption into the field of such modern devices as the mine detector, there was very little buried treasure left to find. Of late, the troves revealed by those under the governments of OCH and BETHOR—with the former of whom in particular lay the bestowal of "a purse springing with gold" —had increasingly turned out to be underseas, or in places like Fort Knox or a Swiss bank, making the recovery of them enterprises so colossal and mischancy as to remove all possibility of profit for client and monastery alike.

On the whole, black magicians had an easier time of it—at least in this life; one must never forget, Father Domenico reminded himself hastily, that they were also damned eternally. It was as mysterious as it had always been that such infernal spirits as LUCIFUGE ROFOCALE should be willing to lend so much power to a mortal whose soul Hell would almost inevitably have won anyhow, considering the character of the average sorcerer, and considering how easily such pacts could be voided at the last instant; and that God would allow so much demonic malice to be vented through the sorcerer upon the innocent. But that was simply another version of the Problem of Evil, for which the Church had long had the answer (or, the dual answer) of free will and original sin.

It had to be recalled, too, that even the practice of white or Transcendental magic was officially a mortal sin, for the modern Church held that all trafficking with spirits—including the un-Fallen, since such dealings inevitably assumed the angels to be demi-urges and other kabbalistic semi-deities—was an abomination, regardless of intent. Once upon a time, it had been recognized that (barring the undertaking of an actual pact) only a man of the highest piety, of the highest purpose, and in the highest state of ritual and spiritual purification, could hope to summon and control a demon, let alone an angel; but there had been too many lapses of intent, and then of act, and in both practicality and compassion the Church had declared all Theurgy to be anathema, reserving unto itself only one negative aspect of magic—exorcism— and that only under the strictest of canonical limitations.

Monte Albano had a special dispensation, to be

sure—partly since the monks had at one time been so spectacularly successful in nourishing the coffers of St. Peter's; partly because the knowledge to be won through the Transcendental rituals might sometimes be said to have nourished the soul of the Rock; and, in small part, because under the rarest of circumstances white magic had been known to prolong the life of the body. But these fountains (to shift the image) were now showing every sign of running dry, and hence the dispensation might be withdrawn at any time— thus closing out the last sanctuary of white magic in the world.

That would leave the field to the black magicians. There were no black sanctuaries, except for the Parisian Brothers of the Left-Hand Way, who were romantics of the school of Éliphas Lévi and were more to be pitied for folly than condemned for evil. But of solitary black sorcerers there were still a disconcerting number—though even one would be far too many.

Which brought Father Domenico directly back to the problem of the letter. He sighed again, turning away from his lectrum and padded off—the Brothers of Monte Albano were discalced—toward the office of the Director, letter in hand. Father Umberto was in (of course he was always *physically* in, like all the rest of them, since the Mount could not be left, once entered, except by the laity and they only by mule-back), and Father Domenico got to the point directly.

"I've had another impassioned screed from our witch smeller," he said. "I am beginning to consider, reluctantly, that the matter is at least as serious as he's been saying all along."

"You mean the matter of Theron Ware, I presume."

"Yes, of course. That American gunmaker we saw went directly from the Mount to Ware, as seemed all too likely even at the time, and Father Uccello says

that there's now every sign of another series of send-
ings being prepared in Positano."

"I wish you could avoid these alliterations. They
make it difficult to discover what you're talking about.
I often feel that a lapse into alliteration or other
grammatical tricks is a sure sign that the speaker isn't
himself quite sure of what he means to say, and is
trying to blind me to the fact. Never mind. As for the
demonolater Ware, we are in no position to interfere
with him, whatever he's preparing."

"The style is Father Uccello's. Anyhow, he insists that
we *must* interfere. He has been practicing divination
—so you can see how seriously *he* takes this, the old
purist—and he says that his principal, whom he takes
great pains not to identify, told him that the meeting
of Ware and Baines presages something truly monstrous for the world at large. According to his information, all Hell has been waiting for this meeting
since the two of them were born."

"I suppose he's sure his principal wasn't in fact a
demon, and didn't slip a lie past him, or at least one
of their usual brags? As you've just indirectly pointed
out, Father Uccello is way out of practice."

Father Domenico spread his hands. "Of course I
can't answer that. Though if you wish, Father, I'll try
to summon Whatever it was myself, and put the
problem to It. But you know how good the chances
are that I'll get the wrong one—and how hard it is to
ask the right question. The great Governors seem to
have no time sense as we understand the term, and as
for demons, well, even when compelled they often
really don't seem to know what's going on outside their
own jurisdictions."

"Quite so," said the Director, who had not himself
practiced in many years. He had been greatly talented
once, but the loss of gifted experimenters to admin-

istrative posts was the curse of all research organizations. "I think it best that you don't jeopardize your own usefulness, and your own soul, of course, in calling up some spirit you can't name. Father Uccello in turn ought to know that there's nothing we can do about Ware. Or does he have some proposal?"

"He wants us," Father Domenico said in a slightly shaky voice, "to impose an observer on Ware. To send one directly to Positano, someone who'll stick to Ware until we know what the deed is going to be. We're just barely empowered to do this—whereas, of course, Father Uccello can't. The question is, do *we* want to?"

"Hmm, hmm," the Director said. "Obviously not. That would bankrupt us—oh, not financially, of course, though it would be difficult enough. But we couldn't afford to send a novice, or indeed anyone less than the best we have, and after the good Lord only knows how many months in that infernal atmosphere . . ."

The sentence trailed off, as the Director's sentences often did, but Father Domenico no longer had any difficulty in completing them. Obviously the Mount could not afford to have even one of its best operators incapacitated—the word, in fact, was "contaminated" —by prolonged contact with the person and effects of Theron Ware. Similarly, Father Domenico was reasonably certain that the Director would in fact send somebody to Positano; otherwise he would not have mounted the obvious objections, but simply dismissed the proposal. For all their usual amusement with Father Uccello, both men knew that there were occasions when one had to take him with the utmost seriousness, and that this was one of them.

"Nevertheless the matter will need to be explored," the Director resumed after a moment, fingering his beads. "I had better give Ware the usual formal notification. We're not obligated to follow up on it, but . . ."

"Quite," Father Domenico said. He put the letter into his scrip and arose. "I'll hear from you, then, when a reply's been received from Ware. I'm glad you agree that the matter is serious."

After another exchange of formalities, he left, head bowed. He also knew well enough who the Director would send, without any intervention of false modesty to cloud the issue; and he was well aware that he was terrified.

He went directly to his conjuring room, the cluttered tower chamber that no one else could use—for magic is intensely sensitive to the personality of the operator—and which was still faintly redolent of a scent a little like oil of lavender, a trace of his last use of the room. *Mansit odor, posses scire duisse deam,* he thought, not for the first time; but he had no intention of summoning any Presence now. Instead, he crossed to the chased casket which contained his 1606 copy—the second edition, but not much corrupted—of the *Enchiridion* of Leo III, that odd collection of prayers and other devices "effectual against all the perils to which every sort and condition of men may be made subject on land, on water, from open and secret enemies, from the bites of wild and rabid beasts, from poisons, from fire, from tempests." For greatest effectiveness he was instructed to carry the book on his person, but he had seldom judged himself to be in sufficient peril to risk so rare and valuable an object, and in any event he did always read at least one page daily, chiefly the *In principio,* a version of the first chapter of the Gospel According to St. John.

Now he took the book out and opened it to the Seven Mysterious Orisons, the only section of the work —without prejudice to the efficacy of the rest of it—

that probably had indeed proceeded from the hand of the Pope of Charlemagne. Kneeling to face the east, Father Domenico, without looking at the page, began the prayer appropriate for Thursday, at the utterance of which, perhaps by no coincidence, it is said that "the demons flee away."

IV

Considerable business awaited Baines in Rome, all the more pressing because Jack Ginsberg was still out of town, and Baines made no special effort to hunt down Jack's report on what the government metallurgist had said about the golden tears amid the mass of other papers. For the time being, at least, Baines regarded the report as personal correspondence, and he had a standing rule never even to open personal letters during office hours, whether he was actually in an office or, as now, working out of a hotel room.

Nevertheless, the report came to the surface the second day that he was back at work; and since he also made it a rule never to lose time to the distractions of an unsatisfied curiosity if an easy remedy was at hand, he read it. The tears on the hankerchief were indeed 24-karat gold; worth about eleven cents, taken together, on the current market, but to Baines representing an enormous investment (or, looked at another way, a potential investment in enormity).

He put it aside with satisfaction and promptly forgot about it, or very nearly. Investments in enormity were his stock in trade; though of late, he thought again with cold anger, they had been paying less and less—hence his interest in Ware, which the other directors of Consolidated Warfare Service would have considered simple insanity. But after all, if the business was no longer satisfying, it was only natural to seek analogous satisfactions somewhere else. An insane man, in Baines' view, would be one who tried to substitute some pleasure—women, philanthropy, art collecting, golf—that offered no cognate satisfaction at all. Baines was ardent about his trade, which was destruction; golf could no more have sublimated that passion than it could have diluted that of a painter or a lecher.

The current fact, which had to be faced and dealt with, was that nuclear weapons had almost totally spoiled the munitions business. Oh, there was still a thriving trade to be drummed up selling small arms to a few small new nations—small arms being defined arbitrarily as anything up to the size of a submarine —but hydrogen fusion and the ballistic missile made the really major achievements of the art, the lubrication of the twenty-year cycle of world wars, entirely too obliterative and self-defeating. These days, Baines' kind of diplomacy consisted chiefly in the fanning of brush fires and civil wars. Even this was a delicate business, for the nationalism game was increasingly an exceedingly confused affair, in which one could never be quite sure whether some emergent African state with a population about the size of Maplewood, N.J., would not turn out to be of absorbing interest to one or more of the nuclear powers. (Some day, of course, they would all be nuclear powers, and then the art would become as formalized and minor as flower arranging.)

The very delicacy of this kind of operation had its satisfactions, in a way, and Baines was good at it. In addition, Consolidated Warfare Service had several thousand man-years of accumulated experience at this sort of thing upon which he could call. One of CWS's chief specialists was in Rome with him now—Dr.

Adolph Hess, famous as the designer of that peculiar all-purpose vehicle called the Hessicopter, but of interest in the present negotiations as the inventor of something nobody was supposed to have heard of—the land torpedo, a rapidly burrowing device that might show up, commendably anonymous, under any installation within two hundred miles of its launching tunnel, geology permitting. Baines had guessed that it might be especially attractive to at least one of the combatants in the Yemeni insurrection, and had proven to be so right that he was now trying hard not to have to dicker with all four of them. This was all the more difficult because, although the two putative Yemeni factions accounted for very little, Nasser was nearly as shrewd as Baines was, and Faisal inarguably a good deal shrewder.

Nevertheless, Baines was not essentially a minaturist, and he was well aware of it. He had recognized the transformation impending in the trade early on, in fact with the publication in 1950 by the U. S. Government Printing Office of a volume titled *The Effects of Atomic Weapons,* and as soon as possible had engaged the services of a private firm called the Mamaroneck Research Institute. This was essentially a brainstorming organization, started by an alumnus of the RAND Corporation, which specialized in imagining possible political and military confrontations and their possible outcomes, some of them so *outré* as to require the subcontracting of free-lance science-fiction writers. From the files of CWS and other sources, Baines fed Mamaroneck materials for its computers, some of which material would have considerably shaken the governments who thought they were sitting on it; and, in return, Mamaroneck fed Baines long, neatly lettered and Xeroxed reports bearing such titles as

"Short- and Long-Term Probabilities Consequent to an Israeli Blockade of the Faeröe Islands."

Baines winnowed out the most obviously absurd of these, but with a care that was the very opposite of conservatism, for some of the strangest proposals could turn out upon second look to be not absurd at all. Those that offered the best combination of surface absurdity with hidden plausibility, he set out to translate into real situations. Hence there was really nothing illogical or even out of character in his interest in Theron Ware, for Baines, too, practiced what was literally an occult art in which the man on the street no longer believed.

The buzzer sounded twice; Ginsberg was back. Baines returned the signal and the door swung open.

"Rogan's dead," Jack said without preamble.

"That was fast. I thought it was going to take Ware a week after he got back from the States."

"It's been a week," Jack reminded him.

"Hmm? So it has. Waiting around for these Ayrabs to get off the dime is hard on the time sense. Well, well. Details?"

"Only what's come over the Reuters ticker, so far. Started as pneumonia, ended as cor pulmonale—heart failure from too much coughing. It appears that he had a small mitral murmur for years. Only the family knew about it, and his physicians assured them that it wasn't dangerous if he didn't try to run a four-minute mile or something like that. Now the guessing is that the last campaign put a strain on it, and the pneumonia did the rest."

"Very clean," Baines said.

He thought about the matter for a while. He had borne the late governor of California no ill will. He had never met the man, nor had any business conflicts with him, and in fact had rather admired his brand of medium-right-wing politics, which had been of the articulate but inoffensive sort expectable of an ex-account executive for a San Francisco advertising agency specializing in the touting of cold breakfast cereals. Indeed, Baines recalled suddenly from the file biography, Rogan had been a fraternity brother of his.

Nevertheless he was pleased. Ware had done the job —Baines was not in the smallest doubt that Ware should have the credit—with great nicety. After one more such trial run, simply to rule out all possibility of coincidence, he should be ready to tackle something larger; possibly, the biggest job of them all.

Baines wondered how it had been done. Was it possible that a demon could appear to a victim in the form of a pneumococcus? If so, what about the problem of reproduction? Well, there had been the appearances all over medieval Europe of fragments of the True Cross, in numbers quantitatively sufficient to stock a large lumberyard. Contemporary clerical apologists had called that Miraculous Multiplication, which had always seemed to Baines to be a classic example of rationalizing away the obvious; but since magic was real, maybe Miraculous Multiplication was too.

These, however, were merely details of technique, in which he made a practice of taking no interest. That kind of thing was for hirelings. Still, it wouldn't hurt to have somebody in the organization who did know something about the technicalities. It was often dangerous to depend solely on outside experts.

"Make out a check for Ware," he told Jack. "From my personal account. Call it a consultation fee— medical, preferably. When you send it to him, set up a date for another visit—let's see—as soon as I get back from Riyadh. I'll take up all this other business with you in about half an hour. Send Hess in, but wait outside."

Jack nodded and left. A moment later, Hess entered silently. He was a tall, bony man with a slight pod, bushy eyebrows, a bald spot in the back, pepper-and-salt hair, and a narrow jaw that made his face look nearly triangular.

"Any interest in sorcery, Adolph? Personal, I mean?"

"Sorcery? I know something about it. For all the nonsense involved, it was highly important in the history of science, particularly the alchemical side, and the astrological."

"I'm not interested in either of those. I'm talking about black magic."

"Then, no, I don't know much about it," Hess said.

"Well, you're about to learn. We're going to visit an authentic sorcerer in about two weeks, and I want you to go along and study his methods."

"Are you pulling my leg?" Hess said. "No, you never do that. Are we going into the business of exposing charlatans, then? I'm not sure I'm the best man for that, Baines. A professional stage magician—a Houdini type—would be far more likely to catch out a faker than I would."

"No, that's not the issue at all. I'm going to ask this man to do some work for me, in his own line, and I need a close observer to see what he does—not to see through it, but to form an accurate impression of the procedures, in case something should go sour with the relationship later on."

"But—well, if you say so, Baines. It does seem rather a waste of time, though."

"Not to me," Baines said. "While you're waiting to talk to the Saudis with me, read up on the subject. By the end of a year I want you to know as much about the subject as an expert. The man himself has told me that that's possible even for me, so it shouldn't tax you any."

"It's not likely to tax my brains much," Hess said drily, "but it may be a considerable tax on my patience. However, you're the boss."

"Right. Get on it."

Hess nodded distantly to Jack as he went out. The two men did not like each other much; in part, Baines sometimes thought, because in some ways they were much alike. When the door had closed behind the scientist, Jack produced from his pocket the waxed-paper envelope that had contained, and obviously still contained, the hankerchief bearing the two transmuted tears.

"I don't need that," Baines said. "I've got your report. Throw that thing away. I don't want anybody asking what it means."

"I will," Jack said. "But first, you'll remember that Ware said that the demon would leave you after two days."

"Sure. Why?"

"Look at this."

Jack took out the handkerchief and spread it carefully on Baines' desk blotter.

On the Irish linen, where the golden tears had been, were now two dull, inarguable smears of lead.

V

By some untraceable miscalculation, Baines' party arrived in Riyadh at the beginning of Ramadan, during which the Arabs fasted all day and were consequently in too short a temper to do business with; which was followed, after twenty-nine solid days, by a three-day feast during which they were too stuporous to do business with. Once negotiations were properly opened, however, they took no more than the two weeks Baines had anticipated.

Since the Moslem calendar is lunar, Ramadan is a movable festival, which this year fell close to Christmas. Baines half suspected that Theron Ware would refuse to see him in so inauspicious a season for servants of Satan, but Ware made no objection, remarking only (by post), "December 25th is a celebration of great antiquity." Hess, who had been reading dutifully, interpreted Ware to mean that Christ had not actually been born on that date—"though in this universe of discourse I can't see what difference that makes," he said. "If the word 'superstition' has any of its old meaning left at all by now, it means that the sign has come to replace the thing—or in other words, that facts come to mean what we say they mean."

"Call it an observer effect," Baines suggested, not entirely jokingly. He was not disposed to argue the

point with either of them; Ware would see him, that
was what counted.

But if the season was no apparent inconvenience to
Ware, it was a considerable one to Father Domenico,
who at first flatly refused to celebrate it in the
very maw of Hell. He was pressed at length and from
both sides by the Director and Father Uccello, whose
arguments had no less force for being so utterly pre-
dictable; and—to skip over a full week of positively
Scholastic disputation—they prevailed, as again he
had been sure they would.

Mustering all his humility, obedience and resignation—his courage seemed to have evaporated—he
trudged forth from the monastery, excused from san-
dals, and mounted a mule, the *Enchiridion* of Leo III
swinging from his neck under his cassock in a new
leather bag, and a selection of his thaumaturgic tools,
newly exorcised, asperged, fumigated and wrapped
in silken cloths, in a satchel balanced carefully on
the mule's neck. It was a hushed leave-taking—all the
more so in its lack of any formalities or even witnesses,
for only the Director knew why he was going, and he
had been restrained with difficulty from bruiting it
about that Father Domenico actually had been ex-
pelled, to make a cover story.

The practical effect of both delays was that Father
Domenico and Baines' party arrived at Ware's palazzo
on the same day, in the midst of the only snowstorm
Positano had seen in seven years. As a spiritual courtesy
—for protocol was all-important in such matters, otherwise neither monk nor sorcerer would have dared to
confront the other—Father Domenico was received
first, briefly but punctiliously; but as a client, Baines
(and his crew, in descending order) got the best quarters. They also got the only service available, since
Ware had no servants who could cross over the invis-

ible line Father Domenico at once ruled at the foot of his apartment door with the point of his bolline.

As was customary in southern Italian towns at this time, three masked kings later came to the gate of the palazzo to bring and ask presents for the children and the Child; but there were no children there and the mummers were turned away, baffled and resentful (for the rich American, who was said to be writing a book about the frescoes of Pompeii, had previously shown himself open-handed), but oddly grateful too; it was a cold night, and the lights in the palazzo were of a grim and distant color.

Then the gates closed. The principals had gathered and were in their places; and the stage was set.

THREE SLEEPS

It requires more courage and intelligence to be a devil than the folk who take experience at hearsay think. And none, save only he who has destroyed the devil in himself, and that by dint of hard work (for there is no other way) knows what a devil is, and what a devil he himself might be, as also what an army for the devils' use are they who think the devils are delusion.
—*The Book of the Sayings of Tsiang Samdup*

VI

Father Domenico's interview with Theron Ware was brief, formal and edgy. The monk, despite his apprehensions, had been curious to see what the magician looked like, and had been irrationally disappointed to find him not much out of the ordinary run of intellectuals. Except for the tonsure, of course; like Baines, Father Domenico found that startling. Also, unlike Baines, he found it upsetting, because he knew the reason for it—not that Ware intended any mockery of his pious counterparts, but because demons, given a moment of inattention, were prone to seizing one by the hair.

"Under the Covenant," Ware told him in excellent Latin, "I have no choice but to receive you, of course, Father. And under other circumstances I might even have enjoyed discussing the Art with you, even though we are of opposite schools. But this is an inconvenient time for me. I've got a very important client here, as you've seen, and I've already been notified that what he wants of me is likely to be extraordinarily ambitious."

"I shan't interfere in any way," Father Domenico said. "Even should I wish to, which obviously I shall, I know very well that any such interference would cost me all my protections."

"I was sure you understood that, but nonetheless

I'm glad to hear you say so," Ware said. "However, your very presence here is an embarrassment—not only because I'll have to explain it to my client, but also because it changes the atmosphere unfavorably and will make my operations more difficult. I can only hope, in defiance of all hospitality, that your mission will be speedily satisfied."

"I can't bring myself to regret the difficulty, since I only wish I could make your operations outright impossible. The best I can proffer you is strict adherence to the truce. As for the length of my stay, that depends wholly on what it is your client turns out to want, and how long *that* takes. I am charged with seeing it through to its conclusion."

"A prime nuisance," Ware said. "I suppose I should be grateful that I haven't been blessed with this kind of attention from Monte Albano before. Evidently what Mr. Baines intends is even bigger than he thinks it is. I conclude without much cerebration that you know something about it I don't know."

"It will be an immense disaster, I can tell you that."

"Hmm. From your point of view, but not necessarily from mine, possibly. I don't suppose you're prepared to offer any further information—on the chance, say, of dissuading me?"

"Certainly not," Father Domenico said indignantly. "If eternal damnation hasn't dissuaded you long before this, I'd be a fool to hope to."

"Well," Ware said, "but you are, after all, charged with the cure of souls, and unless the Church has done another flipflop since the last Congress, it is still also a mortal sin to assume that any man is certainly damned —even me."

That argument was potent, it had to be granted; but Father Domenico had not been trained in casuistry (and that by Jesuits) for nothing.

"I'm a monk, not a priest," he said. "And any information I give you would, on the contrary, almost certainly be used to abet the evil, not turn it aside. I don't find the choice a hard one under the circumstances."

"Then let me suggest a more practical consideration," Ware said. "I don't know yet what Baines intends, but I do know well enough that I am not a Power myself—only a fautor. I have no desire to bite off more than I can chew."

"Now you're just wheedling," Father Domenico said, with energy. "Knowing your own limitations is not an exercise at which I or anyone else can help you. You'll just have to weigh them in the light of Mr. Baines' commission, whatever that proves to be. In the meantime, I shall tell you nothing."

"Very well," Ware said, rising. "I will be a little more generous with my information, Father, than you have been with yours. I will tell you that you will be well advised to adhere to every letter of the Covenant. One step over the line, one toe, and *I shall have you*— and hardly any outcome in this world would give me greater pleasure. I'm sure I make myself clear."

Father Domenico could think of no reply; but none seemed to be necessary.

VII

As Ware had sensed, Baines was indeed disturbed by the presence of Father Domenico, and made a point of bringing it up as the first order of business. After Ware had explained the monk's mission and the Covenant under which it was being conducted, however, Baines felt somewhat relieved.

"Just a nuisance, as you say, since he can't actually intervene," he decided. "In a way, I suppose my bringing Dr. Hess here with me is comparable—he's only an observer, too, and fundamentally he's probably just as hostile to your world-view as this holier-than-us fellow is."

"He's not significantly holier than us," Ware said with a slight smile. "I know something he doesn't know, too. He's in for a surprise in the next world. However, for the time being we're stuck with him— for how long depends upon you. Just what is it you want this time, Dr. Baines?"

"Two things, one depending on the other. The first is the death of Albert Stockhausen."

"The anti-matter theorist? That would be too bad. I rather like him, and besides, some of the work he does is of direct interest to me."

"You refuse?"

"No, not immediately anyhow, but I'm now going

to ask you what I promised I would ask on this occasion. What are you aiming at, anyhow?"

"Something very long-term. For the present, my lethal intentions for Dr. Stockhausen are strictly business-based. He's nibbling at the edges of a scholium that my company presently controls completely. It's a monopoly of knowledge we don't want to see broken."

"Do you think you can keep anything secret that's based in natural law? After the McCarthy fiasco I should have supposed that any intelligent American would know better. Surely Dr. Stockhausen can't be just verging on some mere technicality—something your firm might eventually bracket with a salvo of process patents."

"No, it's in the realm of natural law, and hence not patentable at all," Baines admitted. "And we already know that it can't be concealed forever. But we need about five years' grace to make the best use of it, and we know that nobody else but Stockhausen is even close to it, barring accidents, of course. We ourselves have nobody of Stockhausen's caliber, we just fell over it, and somebody else might do that. However, that's highly unlikely."

"I see. Well . . . the project does have an attractive side. I think it's quite possible that I can persuade Father Domenico that this is the project he came to observe. Obviously it can't be—I've run many like it and never attracted Monte Albano's interest to this extent before—but given sufficient show of great preparations, and difficulty of execution, he might be deluded, and go home."

"That would be useful," Baines agreed. "The question is, could he be deceived?"

"It's worth trying. The task would in fact be difficult —and quite expensive."

"Why?" Jack Ginsberg said, sitting bolt upright in his carved Florentine chair so suddenly as to make his suit squeak against the silk upholstery. "Don't tell us he affects thousands of other people. Nobody ever cast any votes for him that I know of."

"Shut up, Jack."

"No, wait, it's a reasonable question," Ware said. "Dr. Stockhausen does have a large family, which I have to take into account. And, as I've told you, I've taken some pleasure in his company on a few occasions —not enough to balk at having him sent for, but enough to help run up the price.

"But that's not the major impediment. The fact is that Dr. Stockhausen, like a good many theoretical physicists these days, is a devout man—and further-more, he has only a few venial sins to account for, nothing in the least meriting the attention of Hell. I'll check that again with Someone who knows, but it was accurate as of six months ago and I'd be astonished if there's been any change. He's not a member of any formal congregation, but even so he's nobody a demon could reasonably have come for him—and there's a chance that he might be defended against any direct assault."

"Successfully?"

"It depends on the forces involved. Do you want to risk a pitched battle that would tear up half of Düsseldorf? It might be cheaper just to mail him a bomb.

"No, no. And I don't want anything that might look like some kind of laboratory accident—that'd be just the kind of clue that would set everybody else in his field haring after what we want to keep hidden. The whole secret lies in the fact that once Stockhausen knows what we know, he could create a major explosion with—well, with the equivalent of a blackboard and two pieces of chalk. Isn't there any other way?"

"Men being men, there's always another way. In this instance, though, I'd have to have him tempted. I know at least one promising avenue. But he might not fall. And even if he did, as I think he would, it would take several months and a lot of close monitoring. Which wouldn't be altogether intolerable either, since it would greatly help to mislead Father Domenico."

"What would it cost?" Jack Ginsberg said.

"Oh—say about eight million. Entirely a contingent fee this time, since I can't see that there'd be any important out-of-pocket money needed. If there is, I'll absorb it."

"That's nice," Jack said. Ware took no notice of the feeble sarcasm.

Baines put on his adjudicative face, but inwardly he was well satisfied. As a further test, the death of Dr. Stockhausen was not as critical as that of Governor Rogan, but it did have the merit of being in an entirely different social sphere; the benefits to Consolidated Warfare Service would be real enough, so that Baines had not had to counterfeit a motive, which might have been detected by Ware and led to premature further questions; and finally, the objections Ware had raised, while in part unexpected, had been entirely consistent with everything the magician had said before, everything that he appeared to be, everything that his style proclaimed, despite the fact that he was obviously a complex man.

Good. Baines liked consistent intellectuals, and wished that he had more of them in his organization. They were always fanatics of some sort when the chips were down, and hence presented him with some large and easily grasped handle precisely when he had most need of it. Ware hadn't exhibited his handle yet, but he would; he would.

"It's worth it," Baines said, without more than a decorous two seconds of apparent hesitation. "I do want to remind you, though, Dr. Ware, that Dr. Hess here is one of my conditions. I want you to allow him to watch while you operate."

"Oh, very gladly," Ware said, with another smile that, this time, Baines found disquieting; it seemed false, even unctuous, and Ware was too much in command of himself to have meant the falsity not to be noticed. "I'm sure he'll enjoy it. You can all watch, if you like. I may even invite Father Domenico."

VIII

Dr. Hess arrived punctually the next morning for his appointment to be shown Ware's workroom and equipment. Greeting him with a professional nod—"Coals to Newcastle, bringing Mitford and me up here for a tertiary," Hess found himself quoting in silent inanity—Ware led the way to a pair of heavy, brocaded hangings behind his desk, which parted to reveal a heavy brass-bound door of what was apparently cypress wood. Among its fittings was a huge knocker with a face like the mask of tragedy, except that the eyes had cat-like pupils in them.

Hess had thought himself prepared to notice everything and be surprised by nothing, but he was taken aback when the expression on the knocker changed, slightly but inarguably, when Ware touched it. Apparently expecting his startlement, Ware said without looking at him, "There's nothing in here really worth stealing, but if anything were taken it would cost me a tremendous amount of trouble to replace it, no matter how worthless it would prove to the thief. Also, there's the problem of contamination—just one ignorant touch could destroy the work of months. It's rather like a bacteriology laboratory in that respect. Hence the Guardian."

"Obviously there can't be a standard supply house for your tools," Hess agreed, recovering his composure.

"No, that's not even theoretically possible. The operator must make everything himself—not as easy now as it was in the Middle Ages, when most educated men had the requisite skills as a matter of course. Here we go."

The door swung back as if being opened from the inside, slowly and soundlessly. At first it yawned on a deep scarlet gloom, but Ware touched a switch, and, with a brief rushing sound, like water, sunlight flooded the room.

Immediately Hess could see why Ware had rented this particular palazzo and no other. The room was an immense refectory of Sienese design, which in its heyday must often have banquetted as many as thirty nobles; there could not be another half as big in Positano, though the palazzo as a whole was smaller than some. There were mullioned windows overhead, under the ceiling, running around all four walls, and the sunlight was pouring through two ranks of them. They were flanked by pairs of red-velvet drapes, unpatterned, hung from traverse rods; it had been these that Hess had heard pulling back when Ware had flipped the wall switch.

At the rear of the room was another door, a broad one also covered by hangings, which Hess supposed must lead to a pantry or kitchen. To the left of this was a medium-sized, modern electric furnace, and beside it an anvil bearing a hammer that looked almost too heavy for Ware to lift. On the other side of the furnace from the anvil were several graduated tubs, which obviously served as quenching baths.

To the right of the door was a black-topped chemist's bench, complete with sinks, running water and the usual nozzles for illuminating gas, vacuum and compressed air; Ware must have had to install his own pumps for all of these. Over the bench on the back

wall were shelves of reagents; to the right, on the side
wall, ranks of drying pegs, some of which bore contorted pieces of glassware, others, coils of rubber
tubing.

Farther along the wall toward the front was a lectern
bearing a book as big as an unabridged dictionary,
bound in red leather and closed and locked with a
strap. There was a circular design chased in gold on
the front of the book, but at this distance Hess could
not make out what it was. The lectern was flanked by
two standing candlesticks with fat candles in them;
the candles had been extensively used, although there
were shaded electric-light fixtures around the walls,
too, and the small writing table next to the lectern
bore a Tensor lamp. On the table was another book,
smaller but almost as thick, which Hess recognized at
once: the *Handbook of Chemistry and Physics,* forty-
seventh edition, as standard a laboratory fixture as a
test tube; and, a rank of quill pens and inkhorns.

"Now you can see something of what I meant by
requisite skills," Ware said. "Of course I blow much
of my own glassware, but any ordinary chemist does
that. But should I need a new sword, for instance"—
he pointed toward the electric furnace—"I'd have to
forge it myself. I couldn't just pick one up at a costume
shop. I'd have to do a good job of it, too. As a modern
writer says somewhere, the only really serviceable sym-
bol for a sharp sword is a *sharp* sword."

"Uhm," Hess said, continuing to look around.
Against the left wall, opposite the lectern, was a long
heavy table, bearing a neat ranking of objects ranging
in length from six inches to about three feet, all closely
wrapped in red silk. The wrappers had writing on
them, but again Hess could not decipher it. Beside
the table, affixed to the wall, was a flat sword cabinet.
A few stools completed the furnishings; evidently

Ware seldom worked sitting down. The floor was parqueted, and toward the center of the room still bore traces of marks in colored chalks, considerably scuffed, which brought from Ware a grunt of annoyance.

"The wrapped instruments are all prepared and I'd rather not expose them," the magician said, walking toward the sword rack, "but of course I keep a set of spares and I can show you those."

He opened the cabinet door, revealing a set of blades hung in order of size. There were thirteen of them. Some were obviously swords; others looked more like shoemaker's tools.

"The order in which you make these is important, too," Ware said. "because, as you can see, most of them have writing on them, and it makes a difference what instrument does the writing. Hence I began with the uninscribed instrument, this one, the bolline or sickle, which is also one of the most often used. Rituals differ, but the one I use requires starting with a piece of unused steel. It's fired three times, and then quenched in a mixture of magpie's blood and the juice of an herb called foirole."

"The *Grimorium Verum* says mole's blood and pimpernel juice," Hess observed.

"Ah, good, you've been doing some reading. I've tried that, and it just doesn't seem to give quite as good an edge."

"I should think you could get a still better edge by finding out what specific compounds were essential and using those," Hess said. "You'll remember that Damascus steel used to be tempered by plunging the sword into the body of a slave. It worked, but modern quenching baths are a lot better—and in your case you wouldn't have to be constantly having to trap elusive animals in large numbers."

"The analogy is incomplete," Ware said. "It would hold if tempering were the only end in view, or if the operation were only another observance of Paracelsus' rule, *Alterius non sit qui suus esse potest*—doing for yourself what you can't trust others to do. Both are practical ends that I might satisfy in some quite different way. But in magic the blood sacrifice has an additional function—what we might call the tempering of, not just the steel, but also the operator."

"I see. And I suppose it has some symbolic functions, too."

"In goëtic art, everything does. In the same way, as you probably also know from your reading, the forging and quenching is to be done on a Wednesday in either the first or the eighth of the day hours, or the third or the tenth of the night hours, under a full Moon. There is again an immediate practical interest being served here—for I assure you that the planetary hours do indeed affect affairs on Earth—but also a psychological one, the obedience of the operator in every step. The grimoires and other handbooks are at best so confused and contradictory that it's never possible to know completely what steps are essential and what aren't, and research into the subject seldom makes for a long life."

"All right," Hess said. "Go on."

"Well, the horn handle has next to be shaped and fitted, again in a particular way at a particular hour, and then perfected at still another day and hour. By the way, you mentioned a different steeping bath. If you use that ritual, the days and the hours are also different, and again the question is, what's essential and what isn't? Thereafter, there's a conjuration to be recited, plus three salutations and a warding spell. Then the instrument is sprinkled, wrapped and fumigated—not in the modern sense, I mean it's perfumed —and is ready to use. After it's used, it has to be exorcised and rededicated, and that's the difference between the wrapped tools on the table and those hanging here in the rack.

"I won't go into detail about the preparation of the other instruments. The next one I make is the pen of the Art, followed by the inkpots and the inks, for obvious reasons—and, for the same reasons, the burin or graver. The pens are on my desk. This fitted needle here is the burin. The rest, going down the line as they hang here rather than in order of manufacture, are the white-handled knife, which like the bolline is nearly an all-purpose tool . . . the black-handled knife, used almost solely for inscribing the circle . . . the stylet, chiefly for preparing the wooden knives used in tanning . . . the wand or blasting rod, which describes itself . . . the lancet, again self-descriptive . . . the staff, a restraining instrument analogous to a shepherd's . . . and lastly the four swords, one for the master, the other three for his assistants, if any."

With a side-glance at Ware for permission, Hess leaned forward to inspect the writings on the graven instruments. Some of them were easy enough to make out: on the sword of the master, for instance, the word MICHAEL appeared on the pommel, and on the blade, running from point to hilt, ELOHIM GIBOR. On the other hand, on the handle of the white-handled knife was engraved the following:

Hess pointed to this, and to a different but equally baffling inscription that was duplicated on the handles of the stylet and the lancet. "What do those mean?"

"Mean? They can hardly be said to mean anything any more. They're greatly degenerate Hebrew characters, originally comprising various Divine Names. I could tell you what the Names were once, but the characters have no content any more—they just have to be there."

"Superstition," Hess said, recalling his earlier conversation with Baines, interpreting Ware's remark about Christmas.

"Precisely, in the pure sense. The process is as fundamental to the Art as evolution is to biology. Now if you'll step this way, I'll show you some other aspects that may interest you."

He led the way diagonally across the room to the chemist's bench, pausing to rub irritatedly at the chalk marks with the sole of his slipper. "I suppose a modern translation of that aphorism of Paracelsus," he said, "would be 'You just can't get good servants any more.' Not to ply mops, anyhow. . . . Now, most of these reagents will be familiar to you, but some of them are special to the Art. This, for instance, is exorcised water, which as you see I need in great quantities. It has to be river water to start with. The quicklime is for tanning. Some laymen, de Camp for instance, will tell you that 'virgin parchment' simply means parchment that's never been written on before, but that's not so—all the grimoires insist that it must be the skin of a male animal that has never engendered, and the *Clavicula Salomonis* sometimes insists upon unborn parchment, as the caul of a newborn child. For tanning I also have to grind my own salt, after the usual rites are said over it. The candles I use have to be made of the first wax taken from a new hive, and so do my almadels. If I need images, I have to make them of earth dug up with my bare hands and reduced to a paste without any tool. And so on.

"I've mentioned aspersion and fumigation, in other words sprinkling and perfuming. Sprinkling has to be done with an aspergillum, a bundle of herbs like a fagot or *bouquet garni*. The herbs differ from rite to rite and you can see I've got a fair selection here— mint, marjoram, rosemary, vervain, periwinkle, sage, valerian, ash, basil, hyssop. In fumigation the most commonly used scents are aloes, incense, mace, benzoin, storax. Also, it's sometimes necessary to make a stench—for instance in the fumigation of a caul— and I've got quite a repertoire of those."

Ware turned away abruptly, nearly treading on Hess' toes, and strode toward the exit. Hess had no choice but to follow him.

"Everything involves special preparation," he said over his shoulder. "even including the firewood if I want to make ink for pacts. But there's no point in my cataloging things further, since I'm sure you thoroughly understand the principles."

Hess scurried after, but he was still several paces behind the magician when the window drapes swished closed and the red gloom was reinstated. Ware stopped and waited for him, and the moment he was through the door, closed it and went back to his seat behind the big desk. Hess, puzzled, walked around the desk and took one of the Florentine chairs reserved for guests or clients.

"Most illuminating," he said politely. "Thank you."

"You're welcome." Ware rested his elbows on the desk and put his fingertips over his mouth, looking down thoughtfully. There was a sprinkle of perspiration over his brow and shaven head, and he seemed more than usually pale; also, Hess noticed after a moment, he seemed to be trying, without major effort, to control his breathing. Hess watched curiously, wondering what could have upset him. After only a moment, however, Ware looked up at him and volunteered the explanation, with an easy half smile.

"Excuse me," he said. "From apprenticeship on, we're trained to secrecy. I'm perfectly convinced that it's unnecessary these days, and has been since the Inquisition died, but old oaths are the hardest to reason away. No discourtesy intended."

"No offense taken," Hess assured him. "However, if you'd rather rest . . ."

"No, I'll have ample rest in the next three days, and be incommunicado, too, preparing for Dr. Baines' commission. So if you've further questions, now's the time for them."

"Well . . . I have no further technical questions, for the moment. But I am curious about a question Baines asked you during your first meeting—I needn't pretend, I'm sure, that I haven't heard the tape. I wonder, just as he did, what your motivation is. I can see from what you've shown me, and from everything you've said, that you've taken colossal amounts of trouble to perfect yourself in your Art, and that you believe in it. So it doesn't matter for the present whether or not *I* believe in it, only whether or not I believe in *you*. And your laboratory isn't a sham, it isn't there solely for extortion's sake, it's a place where a dedicated man works at something he thinks important. I confess I came to scoff—and to expose you, if I could—and I still can't credit that any of what you do works, or ever did work. But I accept that you so believe."

Ware gave him a half nod. "Thank you; go on."

"I've no further to go but the fundamental question. You don't really need money, you don't seem to collect

art or women, you're not out to be President of the
World or the power behind some such person—and
yet by your lights you have damned yourself eternally
to make yourself expert in this highly peculiar subject.
What on earth *for?*"

"I could easily duck that question," Ware said
slowly. "I could point out, for instance, that under
certain circumstances I could prolong my life to seven
hundred years, and so might not be worrying just yet
about what might happen to me in the next world. Or
I could point out what you already know from the
texts, that every magician hopes to cheat Hell in the
end—as several did who are now nicely ensconced on
the calendar as authentic saints.

"But the real fact of the matter, Dr. Hess, is that I
think what I'm after is worth the risk, and what I'm
after is something you understand perfectly, and for
which you've sold your own soul, or if you prefer an
only slightly less loaded word, your integrity, to Dr.
Baines—*knowledge.*"

"Uhmn. Surely there must be easier ways—"

"You don't believe that. You think there may be
more reliable ways, such as scientific method, but you
don't think they're any easier. I myself have the utmost
respect for scientific method, but I know that it doesn't
offer me the kind of knowledge I'm looking for—
which is also knowledge about the makeup of the
universe and how it is run, but not a kind that any
exact science can provide me with, because the sciences
don't accept that some of the forces of nature are
Persons. Well, but some of them are. And without
dealing with those Persons I shall never know any of
the things I want to know.

"This kind of research is just as expensive as under-
writing a gigantic particle accelerator, Dr. Hess, and
obviously I'll never get any government to underwrite

it. But people like Dr. Baines can, if I can find enough of them—just as they underwrite you.

"Eventually, I may have to pay for what I've learned with a jewel no amount of money could buy. Unlike Macbeth, I know one *can't* 'skip the life to come.' But even if it does come to that, Dr. Hess—and probably it will—I'll take my knowledge with me, and it will have been worth the price.

"In other words—just as you suspected—I'm a fanatic."

To his own dawning astonishment, Hess said slowly:

"Yes. Yes, of course . . . so am I."

IX

Father Domenico lay in his strange bed on his back, staring sleeplessly up at the pink stucco ceiling. Tonight was the night he had come for. Ware's three days of fasting, lustration and prayer—surely a blasphemous burlesque of such observances as the Church knew them, in intent if not in content—were over, and he had pronounced himself ready to act.

Apparently he still intended to allow Baines and his two repulsive henchmen to observe the conjuration, but if he had ever had any intention of including Father Domenico in the ceremony, he had thought better of it. That was frustrating, as well as a great relief; but, in his place, Father Domenico would have done the same thing.

Yet even here, excluded from the scene and surrounded by every protection he had been able to muster, Father Domenico could feel the preliminary oppression, like the dead weather before an earthquake. There was always a similar hush and tension in the air just before the invocation of one of the Celestial Powers, but with none of these overtones of maleficence and disaster . . . or would someone ignorant of what was actually proposed be able to tell the difference? That was a disquieting thought in itself, but one that could practically be left to Bishop Berkeley and the logical Positivists. Father Domenico knew what was going on—a ritual of supernatural murder; and could not help but tremble in his bed.

Somewhere in the palazzo there was the silvery sound of a small clock striking, distant and sweet. The time was now 10:00 P.M., the fourth hour of Saturn on the day of Saturn, the hour most suitable—as even the blameless and pitiable Peter de Abano had written—for experiments of hatred, enmity and discord; and Father Domenico, under the Covenant, was forbidden even to pray for failure.

The clock, that two-handed engine that stands behind the Door, struck, and struck no more, and Ware drew the brocaded hangings aside.

Up to now, Baines, despite himself, had felt a little foolish in the girdled white-linen garment Ware had insisted upon, but he cheered up upon seeing Jack Ginsberg and Dr. Hess in the same vestments. As for Ware, he was either comical or terrible, depending upon what view one took of the proceedings, in his white Levite surcoat with red-silk embroidery on the breast, his white-leather shoes lettered in cinnabar, and his paper crown bearing the word EL. He was girdled with a belt about three inches wide, which seemed to have been made from the skin of some hairy, lion-colored animal. Into the girdle was thrust a red-wrapped, scepter-like object, which Baines identified tentatively from a prior description of Hess' as the wand of power.

"And now we must vest ourselves," Ware said, almost in a whisper. "Dr. Baines, on the desk you will find three garments. Take one, and then another and another. Give two to Dr. Hess and Mr. Ginsberg. Don the other yourself."

Baines picked up the huddle of cloth. It turned out to be an alb.

"Take up your vestments and lift them in your hands above your heads. At the amen, let them fall. Now:

"ANTON, AMATOR, EMITES, THEODONIEL, PONCOR, PAGOR, ANITOR, *by the virtue of these most holy angelic names do I clothe myself, O Lord of Lords, in my Vestments of Power, that so I may fulfill, even unto their term, all things which I desire to effect through Thee,* IDEODANIACH, PAMOR, PLAIOR, *Lord of Lords, Whose kingdom and rule endureth forever and ever. Amen."*

The garments rustled down, and Ware opened the the door.

The room beyond was only vaguely lit with yellow candlelight, and at first bore almost no resemblance to the chamber Dr. Hess had described to Baines. As his eyes accommodated, however, Baines was gradually able to see that it was the same room, its margins now indistinct and its furniture slightly differently ordered: only the lectern and the candlesticks—there were now four of them, not two—were moved out from the walls and hence more or less visible.

But it was still confusing, a welter of flickering shadows and slightly sickening perfume, most unlike the blueprint of the room that Baines had erected in his mind from Hess' drawing. The thing that dominated the real room itself was also a drawing, not any piece of furniture or detail of architecture: a vast double circle on the floor in what appeared to be whitewash. Between the concentric circles were written innumerable words, or what might have been words, in characters which might have been Hebrew, Greek, Etruscan or even Elvish for all Baines could tell. Some few were in Roman lettering, but they, too, were names he could not recognize; and around the outside of the outer circle were written astrological signs in their zodiacal order, but with Saturn to the north.

At the very center of this figure was a ruled square about two feet on a side, from each corner of which proceeded chalked, conventionalized crosses, which did not look in the least Christian. Proceeding from each of these, but not connected to them, were four six-pointed stars, verging on the innermost circle. The stars at the east, west and south each had a Tau scrawled at their centers; presumably the Saturnmost did too, but if so it could not be seen, for the heart of that emplacement was hidden by what seemed to be a fat puddle of stippled fur.

Outside the circles, at the other compass points, were drawn four pentagrams, in the chords of which were written TE TRA GRAM MA TON, and at the centers of which stood the candles. Farthest away from all this —about two feet outside the circle and three feet over it to the north—was a circle enclosed by a triangle, also much lettered inside and out; Baines could just see that the characters in the angles of the triangle read NI CH EL.

"Tanists," Ware whispered, pointing into the circle, "take your places."

He went toward the long table Hess had described and vanished in the gloom. As instructed, Baines walked into the circle and stood in the western star; Hess followed, taking the eastern; and Ginsberg, very slowly, crept into the southern. To the north, the puddle of fur revolved once widdershins and resettled itself with an unsettling sigh, making Jack Ginsberg jump. Baines inspected it belatedly. Probably it was only a cat, as was supposed to be traditional, but in this light it looked more like a badger. Whatever it was, it was obscenely fat.

Ware reappeared, carrying a sword. He entered the circle, closed it with the point of the sword, and proceeded to the central square, where he lay the sword across the toes of his white shoes; then he drew the wand from his belt and unwrapped it, laying the red-silk cloth across his shoulders.

"From now on," he said, in a normal, even voice, "no one is to move."

From somewhere inside his vestments he produced a small crucible, which he set at his feet before the recumbent sword. Small blue flames promptly began to rise from the bowl, and Ware cast incense into it. He said:

"Holocaust. Holocaust. Holocaust."

The flames in the brazier rose slightly.

"We are to call upon MARCHOSIAS, a great marquis of the Descending Hierarchy," Ware said in the same conversational voice. "Before he fell, he belonged to the Order of Dominations among the angels, and thinks to return to the Seven Thrones after twelve hundred years. His virtue is that he gives true answers. Stand fast, all."

With a sudden motion, Ware thrust the end of his rod into the surging flames of the brazier. At once the air of the hall rang with a long, frightful chain of woeful howls. Above the bestial clamor, Ware shouted:

"I adjure thee, great MARCHOSIAS, as the agent of the Emperor LUCIFER, and of his beloved son LUCIFAGE ROFOCALE, by the power of the pact I have with thee, and by the Names ADONAY, ELIOM, JEHOVAM, TAGLA, MATHON, ALMOUZIN, ARIOS, PITHONA, MAGOTS, SYLPHAE, TABOTS, SALAMANDRAE, GNOMUS, TERRAE, COELIS, GODENS, AQUA, and by the whole hierarchy of superior intelligences who shall constrain thee against thy will, *venite, venite, submiritillor* MARCHOSIAS!"

The noise rose higher, and a green steam began to come off the brazier. It smelt like someone was burning hart's horn and fish gall. But there was no other answer. His face white and cruel, Ware rasped over the tumult:

"I adjure thee, MARCHOSIAS, by the pact, and by the Names, appear instanter!" He plunged the rod a second time into the flames. The room screamed; but still there was no apparition.

"Now I adjure thee, LUCIFUGE ROFOCALE, whom I command, as the agent of the Lord and Emperor of Lords, send me thy messenger MARCHOSIAS, forcing him to forsake his hiding place, wheresoever it may be, and warning thee—"

The rod went back in the fire. Instantly, the palazzo rocked as though the earth had moved under it.

"Stand fast!" Ware said hoarsely.

Something Else said.

HUSH, I AM HERE. WHAT DOST THOU SEEK OF ME? WHY DOST THOU DISTURB MY REPOSE? LET MY FATHER REST, AND HOLD THY ROD.

Never had Baines heard a voice like that before. It seemed to speak in syllables of burning ashes.

"Hadst thou appeared when first I invoked thee, I had by no means smitten thee, nor called thy father," Ware said. "Remember, if the request I make of thee be refused, I shall thrust again my rod into the fire."

THINK AND SEE!

The palazzo shuddered again. Then, from the middle of the triangle to the northwest, a slow cloud of yellow fumes went up toward the ceiling, making them all cough, even Ware. As it spread and thinned, Baines could see a shape forming under it; but he found it impossible to believe. It was—it was something like a she-wolf, gray and immense, with green and glistening eyes. A wave of coldness was coming from it.

The cloud continued to dissipate. The she-wolf

glared at them, slowly spreading her griffin's wings. Her serpent's tail lashed gently, scalily.

In the northern pentacle, the great Abyssinian cat sat up and stared back. The demon-wolf showed her teeth and emitted a disgusting belch of fire. The cat settled its front feet indifferently.

"Stand, by the Seal," Ware said. "Stand and transform, else I shall plunge thee back whence thou camest. I command thee."

The she-wolf vanished, leaving behind in the triangle a plump, modest-looking young man wearing a decorous necktie, a dildo almost as long and nothing else. "Sorry, boss," he said in a sugary voice. "I had to try, you know. What's up?"

"Don't try to wheedle me, vision of stupidity," Ware said harshly. "Transform, I demand of thee, thou'rt wasting thy father's time, and mine! Transform!"

The young man stuck out his tongue, which was copper-green. A moment later, the triangle was occupied by a black-bearded man apparently twice his age, wearing a forest-green robe trimmed in ermine and a glittering crown. It hurt Baines' eyes to look at it. An odor of sandalwood began slowly to diffuse through the room.

"That's better," Ware said. "Now I charge thee, by those Names I have named and on pain of those torments thou hast known, to regard the likeness and demesne of that mortal whose eidolon I hold in my mind, and that when I release thee, thou shalt straightaway go unto him, not making thyself known unto him, but revealing, as it were to come from his own intellectual soul, a vision and understanding of that great and ultimate Nothingness which lurks behind those signs he calls matter and energy, as thou wilt see it in his private forebodings, and that thou remainest with him and deepen his despair without remittal, until such time as he shall despise his soul for its endeavors, and destroy the life of his body."

"I cannot give thee," the crowned figure said, in a voice deep but somehow lacking all resonance, "what thou requirest."

"Refusal will not avail thee," Ware said, "for either shalt thou go incontinently and perform what I command, or I shall in no wise dismiss thee, but shall keep thee here unto my life's end, and torment thee daily, as thy father permitteth."

"Thy life itself, though it last seven hundred years, is but a day to me," said the crowned figure. Sparks issued from its nostrils as it spoke. "And thy torments but a farthing of those I have endured since ere the cosmic egg was hatched, and Eve invented."

For answer, Ware again stabbed the rod into the fire, which, Baines noted numbly, failed even to scorch it. But the crowned figure threw back its bearded head and howled desolately. Ware withdrew the rod, but only by a hand's breadth.

"I shall do as thou commandest," the creature said sullenly. Hatred oozed from it like lava.

"Be it not performed exactly, I shall call thee up again," Ware said. "But be it executed, for thy pay thou shalt carry off the immortal part of the subject thou shalt tempt, which is as yet spotless in the sight of Heaven, and a great prize."

"But not yet enough," said the demon. "For thou must give me also somewhat of thine hoard, as it is written in the pact."

"Thou art slow to remember the pact," Ware said. "But I would deal fairly with thee, knowing marquis. Here."

He reached into his robe and drew out something minute and colorless, which flashed in the candlelight.

At first, Baines took it to be a diamond, but as Ware held it out, he recognized it as an opalescent, crystal tear vase, the smallest he had ever seen, stopper, contents and all. This Ware tossed, underhand, out of the circle to the fuming figure, which to Baines' new astonishment—for he had forgotten that what he was really looking at had first exhibited as a beast— caught it skillfully in its mouth and swallowed it.

"Thou dost only tantalize MARCHOSIAS," the Presence said. "When I have thee in Hell, magician, then shall I drink thee dry, though thy tears flow never so copiously."

"Thy threats are empty. I am not marked for thee, shouldst thou see me in Hell forthever," Ware said. "Enough, ungrateful monster. Cease thy witless plaudering and discharge thine errand. I dismiss thee."

The crowned figure snarled, and then, suddenly, reverted to the form in which it had first showed itself. It vomited a great gout of fire, but the surge failed to pass the wall of the triangle; instead, it collected in a ball around the demon itself. Nevertheless, Baines could feel the heat against his face.

Ware raised his wand.

The floor inside the small circle vanished. The apparition clashed its brazen wings and dropped like a stone. With a rending thunderclap, the floor healed seamlessly.

Then there was silence. As the ringing in Baines' ears died away, he became aware of a distant thrumming sound, as though someone had left a car idling in the street in front of the palazzo. Then he realized what it was: the great cat was purring. It had watched the entire proceedings with nothing more than grave interest. So, apparently, had Hess. Ginsberg seemed to be jittering, but he was standing his ground. Although he had never seen Jack rattled before, Baines could hardly blame him; he himself felt sick and giddy, as though just the effort of looking at MARCHO-SIAS had been equivalent to having scrambled for days up some Himalayan glacier.

"It is over," Ware said in a gray whisper. He looked very old. Taking up his sword, he cut the diagram with it. "Now we must wait. I will be in seclusion for two weeks. Then we will consult again. The circle is open. You may leave."

Father Domenico heard the thunderclap, distant and muffled, and knew that the sending had been made—and that he was forbidden, now as before, even to pray for the soul of the victim (or the patient, in Ware's antiseptic Aristotelian terminology). Sitting up and swinging his feet over the edge of the bed, breathing with difficulty in the musky detumescent air, he walked unsteadily to his satchel and opened it.

Why—that was the question—did God so tie his hands, why did He allow such a compromise as the Covenant at all? It suggested, at least, some limitation in His power unallowable by the firm dogma of Omnipotence, which it was a sin even to question; or, at worst, some ambiguity in His relationship wth Hell, one quite outside the revealed answers to the Problem of Evil.

That last was a concept too terrible to bear thinking about. Probably it was attributable purely to the atmosphere here; in any event, Father Domenico knew that he was in no spiritual or emotional condition to examine it now.

He could, however, examine with possible profit a minor but related question: Was the evil just done the evil Father Domenico had been sent to oversee?

There was every immediate reason to suppose that it was—and if it was, then Father Domenico could go home tomorrow, ravaged but convalescent.

On the other hand, it was possible—dreadful, but in a way also hopeful—that Father Domenico had been commanded to Hell-mouth to await the emission of something worse. That would resolve the puzzling anomaly that Ware's latest undertaking, abominable though they all were, was for Ware not unusual. Much more important, it would explain, at least in part, why the Covenant existed at all: in Tolstoy's words, "God sees the truth, but waits."

And this question, at least, Father Domenico need not simply ponder, but could actively submit to the Divine guidance, even here, even now, provided that he call upon no Presences. That restriction was not prohibitive; what was he a magician for, if not to be as subtle in his works as in his praise?

Inkhorn, quill, straightedge, three different discs of different sizes cut from virgin cardboard—not an easy thing to come by—and the wrapped burin came out of the satchel and were arranged on top of his dresser, which would serve well enough for a desk. On the cardboard discs he carefully inscribed three different scales: the A camerae of sixteen divine attributes from *bonitas* to *patientia;* the T camerae of thirty attributes of things, from *temporis* to *negatio;* and the E camerae of the nine questions, from *whether* to *how great.* He centerpunched all three discs with the burin, pinned them together with a cuff link and finally asperged the assembled Lull Engine with holy water from the satchel. Over it he said:

"I conjure thee, O form of this instrument, by the authority of God the Father Almighty, by the virtue of Heaven and the stars, by that of the elements, by

that of stones and herbs, and in like manner by the
virtue of snowstorms, thunder and winds, and belike
also by the virtue of the *Ars magna* in whose figure
thou art drawn, that thou receive all power unto the
performance of those things in the perfection of which
we are concerned, the whole without trickery, false-
hood or deception, by the command of God, Creator
of the Angels and Emperor of the Ages. DAMAHII, LU-
MECH, GADAL, PANCIA, VELOAS, MEOROD, LAMIDOCH,
BALDACH, ANERETHON, MITRATON, most holy angels, be
ye wardens of this instrument. *Domine, Deus meus, in
te speravi. . . . Confitebor tibi, Domine, in toto corde
meo. . . . Quemadmodum desiderat cervus ad fontes
aquarum. . . .* Amen."

This said, Father Domenico took up the engine and
turned the circles against each other. Lull's great art
was not easy to use; most of the possible combinations
of any group of wheels were trivial, and it took reason
to see which were important, and faith to see which
were inspired. Nevertheless, it had one advantage
over all other forms of scrying: it was not, in any strict
sense, a form of magic.

He turned the wheels at random the required number of times, and then, taking the outermost by its
edge, shook it to the four quarters of the sky. He was
almost afraid to look at the result.

But on that very first essay, the engine had generated:

PATIENCE/BECOMING/REALITY

It was the answer he had both feared and hoped
for. And it was, he realized with a subdued shock,
the only answer he could have expected on Christmas
Eve.

He put the engine and the tools back in his satchel,
and crept away into the bed. In his state of over-

exhaustion and alarm, he did not expect to sleep . . . but within two turns of the glass he was no longer in the phenomenal world, but was dreaming instead that, like Gerbert the magician-Pope, he was fleeing the Holy Office down the wind astride a devil.

X

Ware's period of recovery did not last quite as long as he had prophesied. He was visibly up and about by Twelfth Night. By that time, Baines—though only Jack Ginsberg could see and read the signs—was chafing at the inaction. Jack had to remind him that in any event at least two months were supposed to pass before the suicide of Dr. Stockhausen could even be expected, and suggested that in the interim they all go back to Rome and to work.

Baines shrugged the suggestion off. Whatever else was on his mind, it did not seem to involve Consolidated Warfare Service's interests more than marginally . . . or, at least, the thought of business could not distract him beyond the making of a small number of daily telephone calls.

The priest or monk or whatever he was, Father Domenico, was still in attendance too. Evidently he had not been taken in by the show. Well, that was Ware's problem, presumably. All the same, Jack stayed out of sight of the cleric as much as possible; having him around, Jack recalled in a rare burst of association with his Bronx childhood, was a little like being visited by a lunatic Orthodox relative during a crucial marriage brokerage.

Not so lunatic at that, though; for if magic really worked—as Jack had had to see that it did—then

the whole tissue of metaphysical assumptions Father
Domenico stood for, from Moses through the kab-
balah to the New Testament, had to follow, as a
matter of logic. After this occurred to Jack, he not
only hated to see Father Domenico, but had night-
mares in which he felt that Father Domenico was
looking back at him.

Ware himself, however, did not emerge officially, to
be talked to, until his predicted fourteenth day. Then,
to Jack's several-sided disquietude, the first person he
called into his office was Jack Ginsberg.

Jack wanted to talk to Ware only slightly more
than he wanted to talk to the barefooted, silently
courteous Father Domenico; and the effect upon
Baines of Ware's singling Jack out for the first post-
conjuration interview, though under ordinary circumstances it could have been discounted as minor, could
not even be conjectured in Baines' present odd state
of mind. After a troubled hour, Jack took the problem to Baines, not even sure any more of his own
delicacy in juggling such an egg.

"Go ahead," was all Baines said. He continued to
give Jack the impression of a man whose mind was
not to be turned more than momentarily from some
all-important thought. That was alarming, too, but
there seemed to be nothing to be done about it. Setting his face into its business mold of pleasant atten-
tiveness, over slightly clenched teeth, Jack marched up
to Ware's office.

The sunlight there was just as bright and innocent
as ever, pouring directly in from the sea-sky on top
of the cliff. Jack felt slightly more in contact with what
he had used to think of as real life. In some hope of
taking the initiative away from Ware and keeping it,
he asked the magician, even before sitting down, "Is
there some news already?"

"None at all," Ware said. "Sit down, please. Dr. Stockhausen is a tough patient, as I warned you all at the beginning. It's possible that he won't fall at all, in which case a far more strenuous endeavor will be required. But in the meantime I'm assuming that he will, and that I therefore ought to be preparing for Dr. Baines' next commission. That's why I wanted to see you first."

"I haven't any idea what Dr. Baines' next commission is," Jack said. "and if I did I wouldn't tell you before he did."

"You have a remorselessly literal mind, Mr. Ginsberg. I'm not trying to pump you. I already know, and it's enough for the time being, that Mr. Baines' next commission will be something major—perhaps even a unique experiment in the history of the Art. Father Domenico's continued presence here suggests the same sort of thing. Very well, if I'm to tackle such a project, I'll need assistants—and I have no remaining apprentices. They become ambitious very early and either make stupid technical mistakes or have to be dismissed for disobedience. Laymen, even sympathetic laymen, are equally mischancy, simply because of their eagerness and ignorance. But if they're highly intelligent, it's sometimes safe to use them. Sometimes. Given those disclaimers, that explains why I allowed you *and* Dr. Hess to watch the Christmas Eve affair, not just Dr. Hess, whom Dr. Baines had asked for, and why I want to talk to you now."

"I see," Jack said, "I suppose I should be flattered."

Ware sat back in his chair and raised his hands as if exasperated. "Not at all. I see that I'd better be blunt. I was quite satisfied with Dr. Hess' potentialities and so don't need to talk to him any more, except to instruct him. But I am none too happy with yours. You strike me as a weak reed."

"I'm no magician," Jack said, holding onto his temper. "If there's some hostility between us, it's only fair to recognize that I'm not its sole cause. You went out of your way to insult me at our very first interview, only because I was normally suspicious of your pretensions, as I was supposed to be, on behalf of my job. I'm not easily offended, Dr. Ware, but I'm more cooperative if people are reasonably polite to me."

"*Stercor*," Ware said. The word meant nothing to Jack. "You keep thinking I'm talking about public relations, and getting along with people, and all that goose grease. Far from it. A little hatred never hurts the Art, and studied insult is valuable in dealing with demons—there are only a few who can be flattered to any profit, and the man who can be flattered isn't a man at all, he's a dog. Do try to understand me, Mr. Ginsberg. What I'm talking about is neither your footling hostility nor your unexpectedly slow brains, but your rabbit's courage. There was a moment during the last ceremony when I could see that you were going to step out of your post. You didn't know it, but I had to paralyze you, and I saved your life. If you had moved you would have endangered all of us, and had that happened I would have thrown you to MARCHOSIAS like an old bone. It wouldn't have saved the purpose of the ceremony, but it would have kept the demon from gobbling up everybody else but Ahktoi."

"Ach . . . ?"

"My familiar. The cat."

"Oh. Why not the cat?"

"He's on loan. He belongs to another demon—my patron. Do stop changing the subject, Mr. Ginsberg. If I'm going to trust you as a Tanist in a great work, I'm going to have to be reasonably sure that you'll stand fast when I tell you to stand fast, no matter what you see or hear, and that when I ask you to take some small part in the ritual, you'll do it accurately and punctually. Can you assure me of this?"

"Well," Jack said earnestly, "I'll do my best."

"But what for? Why do you want to sell me? I don't know what you mean by your 'best' until I know what's in it for you, besides just keeping you your job—or making a good impression on me because it's a reflex with you to make a good impression on people. Explain this to me, please! I know that there's something in this situation that hits you where you live. I could see that from the outset, but my first guess as to what it was evidently was wrong, or anyhow not central. Well, what *is* central to you? The situation has now ripened to the point when you're going to have to tell me what it is. Otherwise I shall shut you out, and that will be that."

Wobbling between unconventional hope and standard caution, Jack pushed himself out of the Florentine chair and toe-heel-toed to the window, adjusting his tie automatically. From this height, the cliff-clinging apartments of Positano fell away to the narrow beach like so many Roman tenements crowded with deposed kings—and with beach boys hoping to pick up an American heiress for the season. Except for the curling waves and a few distant birds, the scene was motionless, yet somehow to Jack it seemed to be slowly, inexorably sliding into the sea.

"Sure, I like women," he said in a low voice. "And I've got special preferences I don't find it easy to satisfy, even with all the money I make. For one thing, in my job I'm constantly working with classified material—secrets—either some government's or the company's. That means I don't dare put myself into a position where I could be blackmailed."

"Which is why you refused my offer when we first

talked," Ware said. "That was discreet, but unnecessary. As you've probably realized by now, neither spying nor extortion has any attraction for me—the potential income from either or both would be a pittance to me."

"Yes, but I won't always have you around," Jack said, turning back toward the desk. "And I'd be stupid to form new tastes that only you could keep supplied."

" 'Pander to' is the expression. Let's be precise. Nevertheless, you have some remedy in mind. Otherwise you wouldn't be being even this frank."

"Yes . . . I do. It occurred to me when you agreed to allow Hess to tour your laboratory." He was halted by another stab of jealousy, no less acute for being half reminiscent. Drawing a deep breath, he went on, "I want to learn the Art."

"Oho. That *is* a reversal."

"You said it was possible," Jack said in a rush, emboldened by a desperate sense of having now nothing to lose. "I know you said you don't take apprentices, but I wouldn't be trying to stab you in the back or take over your clients, I'd only be using the Art for my specialized purposes. I couldn't pay you any fortune, but I do have money. I could do the reading in my spare time, and come back after a year or so for the actual instruction. I think Baines would give me a sabbatical for that—he wants somebody on his staff to know the Art, at least the theory, only he thinks it's going to be Hess. But Hess will be too busy with his own sciences to do a thorough job of it."

"You really hate Dr. Hess, don't you?"

"We don't impinge," Jack said stiffly. "Anyhow what I say is true. I could be a lot better expert from Baines' point of view than Hess ever could."

"Do you have a sense of humor, Mr. Ginsberg?"

"Certainly. Everybody does."

"Untrue," Ware said. "Everybody claims to have, that's all. I ask only because the first thing to be sacrificed to the Art is the gift of laughter, and some people would miss it more than others. Yours seems to be residual at best. In you it would probably be a minor operation, like an appendectomy."

"You don't seem to have lost yours."

"You confuse humor with wit, like most people. The two are as different as creativity and scholarship. However, as I say, in your case it's not a great consideration, obviously. But there may be greater ones. For example, what tradition I would be training you in. For instance, I could make a kabbalistic magician of you, which would give you a substantial grounding in white magic. And for the black, I could teach you most of what's in the *Clavicle* and the *Lemegeton*, cutting out the specifically Christian accretions. Would that content you, do you think?"

"Maybe, if it met my primary requirements," Jack said. "But if I had to go on from there, I wouldn't care. These days I'm a Jew only by birth, not by culture—and up until Christmas Eve I was an atheist. Now I don't know what I am. All I know is, I've got to believe what I see."

"Not in this Art," Ware said. "But we'll think of you as a *tabula rasa* for the time being. Well Mr. Ginsberg, I'll consider it. But before I decide, I think you ought to explore further your insight about special tastes becoming satisfiable only through magic, whether mine or yours. You like to think how delightful it would be to enjoy them freely and without fear of consequences, but it often happens—you'll remember Oscar Wilde's epigram on the subject—that fulfilled desire isn't a delight, but a cross."

"I'll take the chance."

"Don't be so hasty. You have no real idea of the risks. Suppose you should find, for example, that no human woman could please you any more, and you'd become dependent on succubi? I don't know how much you know of the theory of such a relationship. In general, the revolt in Heaven involved angels from every order in the hierarchy. And of the Fallen, only those who fell from the lowest ranks are assigned to this sort of duty. By comparison, MARCHOSIAS is a paragon of nobility. These creatures have even lost their names, and there's nothing in the least grand about their malignancy—they are pure essences of narrow meanness and petty spite, the kind of spirit a Sicilian milkmaid calls on to make her rival's toenails split, or give an unfaithful lover a pimple on the end of his nose."

"That doesn't make them sound much different from ordinary women," Jack said, shrugging. "So long as they deliver, what does it matter? Presumably, as a magician I'd have *some* control over how they behaved."

"Yes. Nevertheless, why be persuaded out of desire and ignorance, when an experiment is available to you? In fact, Mr. Ginsberg, I would not trust any resolution you made from the state of simple fantasy you're in now. If you won't try the experiment, I must refuse your petition."

"Wait a minute," Jack said. "Why are you so urgent about this? What kind of advantage do you get out of it?"

"I've already told you that," Ware said patiently. "I will probably need you as a Tanist in Dr. Baines' major enterprise. I want to be able to trust you to stand fast, and I won't be able to do that without being sure of your degree and kind of commitment."

Everything that Ware said seemed to have behind it the sound of doors softly closing in Jack's face. And on the other hand, the possibilities—the opportunities . . .

"What," he said, "do I need to do?"

XI

The palazzo was asleep. In the distance, that same oblivious clock struck eleven; the proper hour of this day, Ware had said, for experiments in venery. Jack waited nervously for it to stop, or for something to begin.

His preparations were all made, but he was uncertain whether any of them had been necessary. After all, if the . . . girl . . . who was to come to him was to be totally amenable to his wishes, why should he have to impress her?

Nevertheless, he had gone through all the special rituals, bathing for an hour, shaving twice, trimming his finger- and toenails and buffing them, brushing his hair back for thirty strokes and combing it with the West German tonic that was said to have allatoin in it, dressing in his best silk pajamas, smoking jacket (though he neither smoked nor drank), ascot and Venetian-leather slippers, adding a dash of cologne and scattering a light film of talcum powder inside the bed. Maybe, he thought, part of the pleasure would be in taking all the trouble and having everything work.

The clock stopped striking. Almost at once there was a slow triple knock at the door, so slow that each soft blow seemed like an independent act. Jack's heart bounded like a boy's. Pulling the sash of his jacket tighter, he said as instructed:

"Come in . . . come in . . . come in."

He opened the door. As Ware had told him to expect, there was no one in the dark corridor outside; but when he closed the door and turned around, there she was.

"Good evening," she said in a light voice with the barest trace of an accent—or was it a lisp? "I am here, as you invited me. Do you like me?"

It was not the same girl who had brought the letter to Ware, so many weeks ago, though she somehow reminded him of someone he had once known, he could not think who. This one was positively beautiful. She was small—half a head shorter than Jack, slender and apparently only about eighteen—and very fair, with blue eyes and a fresh, innocent expression, which was doubly piquant because the lines of her features were patrician, her skin so delicate that it was almost like fine parchment.

She was fully clothed, in spike heels, patterned but otherwise sheer stockings, and a short-sleeved, expensively tailored black dress of some material like rayon, which clung to her breasts, waist and upper hips as though electrified, and then burst into a full skirt like an inverted tulip, breaking just above her knees. Wire-thin silver bracelets slid and tinkled almost inaudibly on her left wrist as she ruffled her chrysanthemum-petal coiffure, and small silver earrings echoed them; between her breasts was a circular onyx brooch inlaid in silver with the word *Cazotte,* set off by a ruby about the size of a fly's eye, the only touch of color in the entire costume; even her makeup was the Italian "white look," long out of style but so exaggerating her paleness as to look almost theatrical on her—almost, but not quite.

"Yes," he said, remembering to breathe.

"Ah, you make up your mind so soon. Perhaps you are wrong." She pirouetted away from him toward the bed, making the black tulip flare, and lace foam under its corolla and around her legs with a dry rustling. She stopped the spin facing him, so suddenly that the skirts snapped above her knees like banners in a stiff gust. She seemed wholly human.

"Impossible," Jack said, mustering all his gallantry. "I think you're exquisite. Uh, what shall I call you?"

"Oh, I do not come when called. You will have to exert yourself more than that. But my name could be Rita, if you need one."

She lifted the front of the skirts up over the welts of her stockings, which cut her white thighs only a few inches beneath the vase of her pelvis, and sat down daintily on the side of the bed. "You are very distant," she said, pouting. "Perhaps you suspect I am only pretty on the outside. That would be unfair."

"Oh no, I'm sure—"

"But how can you be sure yet?" She drew up her heels. "You must come and see."

The clock was striking four when she arose, naked and wet, yet somehow looking as though she was still on high heels, and began to dip up her clothes from the floor. Jack watched this little ballet in a dizziness, half exhaustion and half triumph. He had hardly enough strength left to wiggle a toe, but he had already surprised himself so often that he still had hopes. Nothing had ever been like this before, nothing.

"Must you go?" he said sluggishly.

"Oh yes, I have other business yet."

"Other business? But—didn't you have a good time?"

"A—good time?" The girl turned toward him, stopping in the act of fastening a garter strap. "I am thy servant and thy lamia, Eve-fruit, but thou must not mock me."

"I don't understand," Jack said, struggling to lift his head from the bunched, sweaty pillow.

"Then keep silent." She resumed assembling herself.

"But . . . you seemed . . ."

She turned to him again. "I gave thee pleasure. Congratulate thyself. That is enough. Thou knowest well what I am. I take no pleasure in anything. It is not permitted. Be grateful, and I shall come to thee again. But mock me, and I shall send thee instead a hag with an ass's tail."

"I meant no offense," he said, half sullenly.

"See thou dost not. Thou hadst pleasure with me, that sufficeth. Thou must prove thy virility with mortal flesh. Thy potency, that I go to try even now. It comes on to night i' the other side of the world, and I must plant thy seed before it dies in my fires— if ever it lived at all."

"What do you mean?" he said, in a hoarse whisper.

"Have no fear, I shall be back tomorrow. But in the next span of the dark I must change suit." The dress fell down over the impossibly pliant body. "I become an incubus now, and a woman waits for that, diverted from her husband by the two-fold way. Reach I her in time, thou shalt father a child, on a woman thou shalt never even see. Is that not a wonder? And a fearful child it shall be, I promise thee!"

She smiled at him. Behind her lids now, he saw with nausea and shame, there were no longer any eyes—only blankly flickering lights, like rising sparks in a flue. She was now as fully dressed as she had been at the beginning, and curtsied gravely.

"Wait for me . . . unless, of course, thou dost not want me back tomorrow night . . . ?"

He tried not to answer, but the words came out like clots of poisonous gas.

"Yes . . . oh God . . ."

Cupping both hands over her hidden groin in a gesture of obscene conservatism, she popped into nothingness like a bursting balloon, and the whole weight of the dawn fell upon Jack like the mountains of St. John the Divine.

XII

Dr. Stockhausen died on St. Valentine's day, after three days' fruitless attempts by surgeons from all over the world, even the USSR, to save him from the effects of a draught of a hundred minims of tincture of iodine. The surgery and hospital care were all free; but he died intestate, and it appeared that his small estate— a few royalties from his books and the remains of a ten-year-old Nobel Prize—would be tied up indefinitely; especially in view of the note he left behind, out of which no tribunal, whether scientific or judicial, could hope to separate the mathematics from the ravings for generations to come.

Funds were gathered for his grandchildren and divorced daughter to tide them over; but the last book that he had been writing turned out to be so much like the note that his publishers' referees could think of no colleague to whom it could reasonably be offered for posthumous collaboration. It was said that his brain would be donated to the museum of the Deutsches Akademie in Munich—again only if his affairs could ever be probated. Within three days after the funeral, however, Ware was able to report, both brain and manuscript had vanished.

"MARCHOSIAS may have taken one or both of them," Ware said. "I didn't tell him to, since I didn't want to cause any more suffering to Albert's relatives than was inevitable under the terms of the commission. On the other hand, I didn't tell him not to, either. But the commission itself has been executed."

"Very good," Baines said. He was, in fact, elated. Of the other three people in the office with Ware—for Ware had said there was no way to prevent Father Domenico from attending—none looked as pleased as Baines felt, but after all he was the only man who counted here, the only one to whose emotions Ware need pay any more than marginal attention. "And much faster than you had anticipated, too. I'm very well satisfied, and also I'm now quite ready to discuss my major commission with you, Dr. Ware, if the planets and so on don't make this a poor time to talk about it."

"The planetary influences exert almost no effect upon simple discussion," Ware said, "only on specific preparations—and of course on the experiment itself. And I'm quite rested and ready to listen. In fact, I'm in an acute state of curiosity. Please charge right in and tell me about it."

"I would like to let all the major demons out of Hell for one night, turn them loose in the world with no orders and no restrictions—except of course that they go back by dawn or some other sensible time—and see just what it is they would do if they were left on their own hooks like that."

"Insanity!" Father Domenico cried out, crossing himself. "Now surely the man is possessed already!"

"For once, I'm inclined to agree with you, Father," Ware said, "though with some reservations about the possession question. For all we can know now, it's entirely in character. Tell me this, Dr. Baines, what do you hope to accomplish through an experiment on so colossal a scale?"

"Experiment!" Father Domenico said, his face as white as the dead.

"If you can do no more than echo, Father, I think we'd all prefer that you kept silent—at least until we find out what it is we're talking about."

"I will say what I need to say, when I think it is needful," Father Domenico said angrily. "This thing that you're minimizing by calling it an 'experiment' might well end in the dawn of Armageddon!"

"Then you should welcome it, not fear it, since you're convinced your side must win," Ware said. "But actually there's no such risk. The results may well be rather Apocalyptic, but Armageddon requires the prior appearance of the Antichrist, and I assure you I am not he . . . nor do I see anybody else in the world who might qualify. Now, again, Dr. Baines, what do you hope to accomplish through this?"

"Nothing *through* it," Baines, now totally caught up in the vision, said dreamily. "Only the thing itself—for its aesthetic interest alone. A work of art, if you like. A gigantic action painting, with the world for a canvas—"

"And human blood for pigments," Father Domenico ground out.

Ware held up his hand, palm toward the monk. "I had thought," he said to Baines, "that this was the art you practiced already, and in effect sold the resulting canvasses, too."

"The sales kept me able to continue practicing it," Baines said, but he was beginning to find the metaphor awkward, his though it had originally been. "Look at it this way for a moment, Dr. Ware. Very roughly, there are only two general kinds of men who go into the munitions business—those without consciences, who see the business as an avenue to a great fortune, eventually to be used for something else, like Jack here—and of course there's a subclass of those, people who *do* have consciences but can't resist the money anyhow, or the knowledge, rather like Dr. Hess."

Both men stirred, but apparently both decided not to dispute their portraits.

"The second kind is made up of people like me—people who actually take pleasure in the controlled production of chaos and destruction. Not sadists primarily, except in the sense that every dedicated artist is something of a sadist, willing to countenance a little or a lot of suffering—not only his own, but other people's—for the sake of the end product."

"A familiar type, to be sure," Ware said with a lop-sided grin. "I think it was the saintly Robert Frost who said that a painting by Whistler was worth any number of old ladies."

"Engineers are like this too," Baines said, warming rapidly to his demonstration; he had been thinking about almost nothing else since the conjuration he had attended. "There's a breed I know much better than I do artists, and I can tell you that most of them wouldn't build a thing if it weren't for the kick they get out of the preliminary demolitions involved. A common thief with a gun in his hand isn't half as dangerous as an engineer with a stick of dynamite.

"But in my case, just as in the case of the engineer, the key word is 'controlled'—and, in the munitions business, it's rapidly becoming an obsolete word, thanks to nuclear weapons."

He went on quickly to sketch his dissatisfactions, very much as they had first come to a head in Rome while Governor Rogan was being sent for. "So now you can see what appeals to me about the commission I propose. It won't be a series of mass obliterations under nobody's control, but a whole set of individual actions, each in itself on a comparatively small scale—

and each one, I'm sure, interesting in itself because of all the different varieties of ingenuity and surprise to be involved. And it won't be total because it will also be self-limiting to some small period of time, presumably twelve hours or less."

Father Domenico leaned forward earnestly. "Surely," he said to Ware, "even you can see that no human being, no matter how sinful and self-indulgent, could have elaborated anything so monstrous without the direct intervention of Hell!"

"On the contrary," Ware said, "Dr. Baines is quite right, most dedicated secularists think exactly as he does—only on a somewhat smaller scale. For your further comfort, Father, I am somewhat privy to the affairs of Hell, and I investigate all my major clients thoroughly. I can tell you that Dr. Baines is *not* possessed. But all the same there are still a few mysteries here. Dr. Baines, I still think you may be resorting to too big a brush for the intended canvas, and might get the effects you want entirely without my help. For example, why won't the forthcoming Sino-Russian War be enough for you?"

Baines swallowed hard. "So that's really going to happen?"

"It's written down to happen. It still might not, but I wouldn't bet against it. Very likely it won't be a major nuclear war—three fusion bombs, one Chinese, two Soviet, plus about twenty fission explosions, and then about a year of conventional land war. No other powers are at all likely to become involved. You know this, Dr. Baines, and I should think it would please you. After all, it's almost exactly the way your firm has been trying to pre-set it."

"You're full of consolations today," Father Domenico muttered.

"Well, in fact, I *am* damn pleased to hear it," Baines said. "It isn't often that you plan something that big and have it come off almost as planned. But no, Dr. Ware, it won't be enough for me, because it's still too general and difficult to follow—or will be. I'm having a little trouble with my tenses. For one thing, it won't be sufficiently attributable to me—many people have been working to bring that war about. This experiment will be on my initiative alone."

"Not an insuperable objection," Ware said. "A good many Renaissance artists didn't object to collaborators —even journeymen."

"Well, the spirit of the times has changed, if you want an abstract answer. The real answer is that I *do* object. Furthermore, Dr. Ware, I want to choose my own medium. War doesn't satisfy me any more. It's too sloppy, too subject to accident. It excuses too much."

"?" Ware said with an eyebrow.

"I mean that in time of war, especially in Asia, people expect the worst and try to ride with the punches, no matter how terrible they are. In peacetime, on the other hand, even a small misfortune comes as a total surprise. People complain, 'Why did this have to happen to *me?*'—as though they'd never heard of Job."

"Rewriting Job is the humanist's favorite pastime," Ware agreed. "And his favorite political platform too. So in fact, Dr. Baines, you *do* want to afflict people, just where they're most sensitive to being afflicted, and just when they least expect it, right or wrong. Do I understand you correctly?"

Baines had the sinking feeling that he had explained too much, but there was no help for that now; and, in any event, Ware was hardly himself a saint.

"You do," he said shortly.

"Thank you. That clears the air enormously. One more question. How do you propose to pay for all this?"

Father Domenico surged to his feet with a strangled gasp of horror, like the death throes of an asthmatic.

"You—you mean to do this!"

"Hush. I haven't said so. Dr. Baines, the question?"

"I know I couldn't pay for it in cash," Baines said. "But I've got other assets. This experiment—if it works—is going to satisfy something for me that Consolidated Warfare Service hasn't satisfied in years, and probably never will again except marginally. I'm willing to make over most of my CWS stock to you. Not all of it, but—well—just short of being a controlling interest. You ought to be able to do a lot with that."

"It's hardly enough, considering the risks involved," Ware said slowly. "On the other hand, I've no particular desire to bankrupt you—"

"Dr. Ware," Father Domenico said in an iron voice. "Am I to conclude that you *are* going to undertake this fearful insanity?"

"I haven't said so," Ware replied mildly. "If I do, I shall certainly need your help—"

"Never. *Never!*"

"And everybody else's. It isn't really the money that attracts me, primarily. But without money I should never be able to undertake an experiment like this in the first place, and I'm certain the opportunity will never come up again. If the whole thing doesn't blow up in my face, there'd be an enormous amount to learn from a trial like this."

"I think that's right," Hess' voice said. Baines looked toward him in surprise, but Hess seemed quite serious. "I'd be greatly interested in it myself."

"You'll learn nothing," Father Domenico said, "but

the shortest of all shortcuts to Hell, probably in the body!"

"A negative Assumption?" Ware said, raising both eyebrows this time. "But now you're tempting my pride, Father. There've been only two previous ones in Western history—Johannes Faustus and Don Juan Tenorio. And neither one was properly safeguarded or otherwise prepared. Well, now certainly I must undertake so great a work—provided that Dr. Baines is satisfied that he'll get what he'll be paying for."

"Of course I'm satisfied," Baines said, quivering with joy.

"Not so fast. You've asked me to let all the major demons out of Hell. I can't even begin to do that. I can call up only those with whom I have pacts, and their subordinates. No matter what you have read in Romantic novels and plays, the three superior spirits cannot be invoked at all, and never sign pacts, those being SATHANAS, BEELZEBUTH and SATANACHIA. Under each of these are two ministers, with one of the six of which it is possible to make pacts—one per magician, that is. I control LUCIFUGE ROFOCALE, and he me. Under him in turn, I have pacts with some eighty-nine other spirits, not all of which would be of any use to us here—VASSAGO, for instance, who has a mild nature and no powers except in crystallomancy, or PHOENIX, a poet and teacher. With the utmost in careful preparations, we might involve as many as fifty of the rest, certainly no more. Frankly, I think that will prove to be more than enough."

"I'll cheerfully take your word for it," Baines said promptly. "You're the expert. Will you take it on?"

"Yes."

Father Domenico, who was still standing, swung away toward the door, but Ware's hand shot out toward him above the desk as if to grasp the monk by the nape of the neck. "Hold!" the magician said. "Your commission is *not* discharged, Father Domenico, as you know very well in your heart. You must observe this sending. Even more important, you have already said yourself that it is going to be difficult to keep under control. To that end I demand your unstinting advice in the preparation, your presence in the conjurations, and, should they be needed, your utmost offices in helping me and my other Tanists to abort it. This you cannot refuse—it is all in your mission by stipulation, and in the Covenant by implication. I do not force you to it. I do but remind you of your positive duty to your Lord."

"That . . . is . . . true . . ." Father Domenico said in a sick whisper. His face as gray as an untinted new blotter, he groped for the chair and sat down again.

"Nobly faced. I'll have to instruct everyone here, but I'll start with you, in deference to your obvious distress—"

"One question," Father Domenico said. "Once you've instructed us all, you'll be out of touch with us for perhaps as much as a month to come. I demand the time to visit my colleagues, and perhaps call together a convocation of all white magicians—"

"To prevent me?" Ware said between his teeth. "You can demand no such thing. The Covenant forbids the slightest interference."

"I'm all too horribly aware of that. No, not to interfere, but to stand by, in case of disaster. It would be too late to call for them once you *knew* you were losing control."

"Hmm . . . probably a wise precaution, and one I couldn't justly prevent. Very well. Just be sure you're back when the time comes. About the day, what would you suggest? May Eve is an obvious choice, and we may well need that much time in preparation."

"It's *too* good a time for any sort of control," Father Domenico said grimly. "I definitely do *not* recommend piling a real Walpurgis Night on top of the formal one. It would be wiser to choose an *un*favorable night, the more unfavorable the better."

"Excellent good sense," Ware said. "Very well, then. Inform your friends. The experiment is hereby scheduled for Easter."

With a scream, Father Domenico bolted from the room. Had Baines not been taught all his life long that such a thing was impossible in a man of God, Baines would have identified it without a second thought as a scream of hatred.

XIII

Theron Ware had been dreaming a journey to the
Antartic continent in the midst of its Jurassic splendor,
fifty million years ago, but the dream had been becoming a little muddled with personal fantasies—mostly
involving a minor enemy whom he had in reality sent
for, with flourishes, a good decade ago—and he was
not sorry when it vanished unfinished at dawn.

He awoke sweating, though the dream had not been
especially stressful. The reason was not far to seek:
Ahktoi was sleeping, a puddle of lard and fur, on the
pillow, and had nearly crowded Ware's head off it.
Ware sat up, mopping his pate with the top sheet, and
stared at the cat with nearly neutral annoyance. Even
for an Abyssinian, a big-boned breed, the familiar was
grossly overweight; clearly an exclusive diet of human
flesh was not a healthy regimen for a cat. Furthermore,
Ware was not even sure it was necessary. It was prescribed only in Éliphas Lévi, who often made up such
details as he went along. Certainly PHOENIX, whose
creature Ahktoi was, had made no such stipulation.
On the other hand, it was always best to play safe in
such matters; and, besides, financially the diet was not
much more than a nuisance. The worst that could be
said for it was that it spoiled the cat's lines.

Ware arose, naked, and crossed the cold room to the
lectern, which bore up his Great Book—not the book

of pacts, which was of course still safely in the workroom, but his book of new knowledge. It was open to
the section headed

QUASARS

but except for the brief paragraph summarizing the
reliable scientific information on the subject—a very
brief paragraph indeed—the pages were still blank.

Well, that, like so much else, could wait until
Baines' project was executed. Truly colossal advances
might be made in the Great Book, once all that CWS
money was in the bank.

Ware's retirement had left the members of Baines'
party again at loose ends, and all of them, even Baines,
were probably a little shaken at the magnitude of
what they had contracted for. In Baines and Dr. Hess,
perhaps, there still remained some faint traces of
doubt about its possibility, or at least some inability
to imagine what it would be like, despite the previous
apparition of MARCHOSIAS. No such impediment could
protect Jack Ginsberg, however—not now, when he
awakened each morning with the very taste of Hell in
his mouth. Ginsberg was committed, but he was not
wearing well; he would have to be watched. The waiting period would be especially hard on him. Well, that
couldn't be helped; it was prescribed.

The cat uncurled, yawned, stretched, lurched daintily to its feet and paused at the edge of the bed, peering
down the sideboard as though contemplating the inward slope of Fujiyama. At last it hit the floor with a
double *splat!* like the impacts of two loaded sponges.
There it arched its spine again, stretched out its back
legs individually in an ecstasy of quivering, and walked
slowly toward Ware, its furry abdomen swinging from
side to side. *Hein?* it said in a breathy feminine voice.

"In a minute," Ware said, preoccupied. "You'll get

fed when I do." He had forgotten for the moment that
he had just begun a nine days' fast, which when completed he would enforce also upon Baines and his
henchmen. "Father Eternal, O thou who art seated
upon cherubim and seraphim, who beholdest the
earth and the sea, unto thee do I lift up my hands,
and beseech thine aid alone, thou who art the fulfil-
ment of works, who givest booty unto those who toil,
who exaltest the proud, who art destroyer of all life
the fulfillment of works, who givest booty unto those
who call upon thee. Do thou guard and defend me in
this undertaking, thou who livest and reignest forever
and ever. Amen! Shut up, Ahktoi."

Anyhow it had been years since he had believed for
an instant that Ahktoi was really hungry. Maybe lean
meat was what the cat needed, instead of all that baby
fat—though stillbirths were certainly the easiest kind
of rations to get for him.

Ringing for Gretchen, Ware went into the bath-
room, where he ran a bath, into which he dashed an
ounce of exorcised water left over from the dressing of
a parchment. Ahktoi, who like most Abyssinians loved
running water, leapt up on the rim of the tub and
tried to fish for bubbles. Pushing the cat off, Ware sat
down in the warm pool and spoke the Thirteenth
Psalm, *Dominus illuminatio mea,* of death and resur-
rection, his voice resounding hollowly from the tiles;
adding, "Lord who hast formed man out of nothing to
thine own image and likeness, and me also, unworthy
sinner as I am, deign, I pray thee, to bless and sanctify
this water, that all delusion may depart from me unto
thee, almighty and ineffable, who didst lead forth thy
people from the land of Egypt, and didst cause them
to pass dryshod under the Red Sea, anoint me as thou
wilt, father of sins. Amen."

He slid under the water, crown to toes—but not for

long, for the ounce of exorcised water he had added
still had a trace of quicklime in it from the tanning of
the lambskin, which made his eyes sting. He surfaced,
blowing like a whale, and added quickly to the steamy
air, *"Dixit insipiens in corde suo*—Will you *kindly*
get out of the way, Ahktoi?—who hast formed me in
thine image and in thy likeness, deign to bless and
sanctify this water, so that it may become unto me the
fruition of my soul and body and purpose. Amen."

Hein?"

Someone knocked on the door. His eyes squeezed
closed still, Ware groped his way out. He was met at
the threshold by Gretchen, who sponged his hands and
face ritually with an asperged white cloth, and retreated before him as he advanced into the bedroom.
Now that his eyes were cleared, he could see that she
was naked, but, knowing what she was, that could
scarcely interest him, and, besides, he had been devoted
to celibacy since his earliest love of magic, like anyone
in Orders. Her nakedness was only another rule of the
rite of lustration. Waving her aside, he took three steps
toward the bed, where she had laid out his vestments,
and said to all corners of the phenomenal and epiphe-
nomenal world:

"ASTROSCHIO, ASATH, *á sacra* BEDRIMUBAL, FELUT,
ANABOTOS, SERABILIM, SERGEN, GEMEN, DOMOS, who
art seated above the heavens, who beholdest the
depths, grant me, I pray thee, that those things which
I conceive in my mind may also be executed by me
through thee, who appear clean before thee! Amen."

Gretchen went out, flexing her scabby buttocks, and
Ware began the rite of vesting. *Hein?* Ahktoi said
plaintively, but Ware did not hear. His triduum was
launched, devoutly, in water, and would be observed,
strictly, until the end in blood; wherein would be required to the slaughter a lamb, a dog, a hen and a cat.

THE LAST CONJURATION

There are two equal and opposite errors into which our race can fall about the devils. One is to disbelieve in their existence. The other is to believe, and to feel an excessive or unhealthy interest in them. They themselves are equally pleased by both errors and hail a materialist or a magician with the same delight. . . .

We are really faced with a cruel dilemma. When the humans disbelieve in our existence we lose all the pleasing results of direct terrorism and we make no magicians. On the other hand, when they believe in us, we cannot make them materialists and skeptics. At last not yet. . . . If once we can produce our perfect work—the Materialist Magician, the man, not using, but veritably worshipping, what he vaguely calls "Forces" while denying the existence of "spirits"— then the end of the war will be in sight.

—C. S. Lewis, *The Screwtape Letters*

XIV

Father Domenico found getting north to Monte Albano a relatively easy journey despite all the snow; he was able to take the *rapido* most of the way. Absurdly he found himself worrying about the snow; if it lasted, there would be devastating floods in the spring. But that was not the only affliction the spring had in store.

After the journey, nothing seemed to go right. Only about half of the world's white magicians, a small number in any case, who had been summoned to the convocation had been able to make it, or had thought it worth the trip. One of the greatest, the aged archivist Father Bongfiglioli, had come all the way from Cambridge only to find the rigors of being portaged up the Mount too much for him. He was now in the hospital at the base of the Mount with a coronary infarct, and the prognosis was said to be poor.

Luckily, Father Uccello had been able to come. So had Father Montieth, a venerable master of a great horde of creative (though often ineffectual) spirits of the cislunar sphere; Father Boucher, who had commerce with some intellect of the recent past that was neither a mortal nor a Power, a commerce bearing all the earmarks of necromancy and yet was not; Father Vance, in whose mind floated visions of magics that would not be comprehensible, let alone practicable, for millions of years to come; Father Anson, a brusque engineer type who specialized in unclouding the minds of politicians; Father Selahny, a terrifying kabbalist who spoke in parables and of whom it was said that no one since Leviathan had understood his counsel; Father Rosenblum, a dour, bear-like man who tersely predicted disasters and was always right about them; Father Atheling, a wall-eyed grimoiran who saw portents in parts of speech and lectured everyone in a tense nasal voice until the Director had to exile him to the library except when business was being conducted; and a gaggle of lesser men, and their apprentices.

These and the Brothers of the Order gathered in the chapel of the monastery to discuss what might be done. There was no agreement from the outset. Father Boucher was of the firm opinion that Ware would not be permitted to work any such conjuration on Easter, and that hence only minor precautions were necessary. Father Domenico had to point out that Ware's previous sending—a comparatively minor one to be sure, but what was that saying about the fall of the sparrow?—had been made without a sign of Divine intervention upon Christmas Eve.

Then there was the problem of whether or not to try to mobilize the Celestial Princes and their subordinates. Father Atheling would have it that merely putting these Princes on notice might provoke action against Ware, since there was no predicting what They might do, and hence would be in violation of the Covenant. He was finally outshouted by Fathers Anson and Vance, with the obvious but not necessarily valid argument that the Princes must know all about the matter anyhow.

How shaky that assumption was was revealed that

night, when those bright angels were summoned one by one before the convocation for a council of war. Bright, terrible and enigmatic They were at any time, but at this calling They were in a state of spirit beyond the understanding of any of the masters present in the chapel. ARATRON, chiefest of Them all, appeared to be indeed unaware of the forthcoming unleashing, and disappeared with a roar when it was described. PHALEG, most military of spirits, seemed to know of Ware's plans, but would not discuss them, and also vanished when pressed. OPHEIL the mercurial, too, was preoccupied, as though Ware's plotting were only a negligible distraction from some immensely greater thought; His answers grew shorter and shorter, and He finally lapsed into what, in a mortal, Father Domenico would have unhesitatingly called surliness. Finally—although not intended as final, for the convocation had meant to consult all seven of the Olympians—the water-spirit PHUL when called up appeared fearsomely without a head, rendering converse impossible and throwing the chapel into a perilous uproar.

"These are not good omens," Father Atheling said; and for the first time in his life, everyone agreed with him. It was agreed, also, that everyone except Father Domenico would remain at the Mount through the target day, to take whatever steps then appeared to be necessary; but there was precious little hope that they would be effective. Whatever was going on in Heaven, it appeared to leave small concern to spare for pleas from Monte Albano.

Father Domenico went south again far earlier than he had planned, unable to think of anything but the mystery of that final, decapitate apparition. The leaden skies returned him no answer.

XV

On that penultimate morning, Theron Ware faced the final choice of which demons to call up, and for this he needed to repair to his laboratory, to check the book of pacts. Otherwise his preparations were all made. He had performed the blood sacrifices the previous evening, and then had completely rearranged the furniture in the workroom to accommodate the Grand Circle—the first time he had had need of it in twenty years—the Lesser Circles and the Gateway. There were even special preparations for Father Domenico—who had returned early and with a gratifyingly troubled countenance—should it become necessary to ask the monk to call for Divine intervention; but Ware was tolerably sure it would not be. Though he had never attempted anything of this magnitude before, he felt the work in his fingertips, like a well-practiced sonata.

He was, however, both astonished and disquieted to find Dr. Hess already in the laboratory—not only because of the potentialities for contamination, but at the inevitable conclusion that Hess had worked out how to placate the Guardian of the door. This man evidently was even more dangerous than Ware had guessed.

"Do you want to ruin us all?" Ware demanded.

Hess turned away from the circle he had been inspecting and looked at Ware frankly. He was pale and hollow-eyed; not only had the fasting been hard on his spare frame—that was a hazard every neophyte had to come to terms with—but apparently he had not been sleeping much either. He said at once:

"No indeed. My apologies, Dr. Ware. My curiosity overcame me, I'm afraid."

"You didn't touch anything, I hope?"

"Certainly not. I took your warnings about that with great seriousness, I assure you."

"Well . . . probably no harm done then. I can sympathize with your interest, and even approve it, in part. But I'll be instructing you all in detail a little later in the day, and then you'll have ample time to inspect the arrangements. I do want you to know them intimately. But right now I still have some additional work to do, so if you don't mind . . ."

"Quite." Hess moved obediently toward the door. As he was about to touch the handle, Ware added:

"By the way, Dr. Hess, how *did* you deceive the Guardian?"

Hess made no pretense of being puzzled by the question. "With a white pigeon, and a pocket mirror I got from Jack."

"Hmm. Do you know, that would never have occurred to me. These pagan survivals are mostly a waste of effort. Let's talk about it more, later. You may have something to teach me."

Hess made a small bow and finished his departure. Forgetting him instantly, Ware stared at the Grand Circle for a moment, and then walked around it clockwise to the lectern and unlocked the book of pacts. The stiff pages bent reassuringly in his hands. Each leaf was headed by the character or sign of a demon; below, in the special ink reserved for such high matters—gall, copperas, gum arabic—was the text of

Theron Ware's agreement with that entity, signed at
the bottom by Ware in his own blood, and by the
character of the demon repeated in its own hand.
Leading all the rest was the seal, and also the characters, of Lucifuge Rofocale, which also appeared
on the book's cover:

There then followed eighty-nine others. It was
Ware's sober belief, backed by infernal assurances he
had reason to trust, that no previous magician had
held so many spirits in thrall. After forty years, true,
all the names would change, and Ware would have to
force the re-execution of each pact, and so, again and
again through the five hundred years of life he had
bought from Hagith in his salad days as a white
magician. Nevertheless it could be said that, in the

possession of this book, Ware was at least potentially the wealthiest mortal in all of history, though to anyone else in the world the book would be worth nothing except as a *curiosum*.

These spirits, not counting LUCIFUGE ROFOCALE, comprised the seventeen infernal archangels of the Grand Grimoire, and the seventy-two demons of the Descending Hierarchy once confined in the brazen vessel of Solomon the King: a fabulous haul indeed, and each captive commanding troops and armies of lesser spirits, and damned souls by the thousands of millions, more of them every minute. (For these days, virtually everyone was damned; it had been this discovery that had first convinced Ware that the Rebellion was in fact going to succeed, probably by the year A.D. 2000; the many plain symptoms of chiliastic panic already being manifested amongst the laity were almost certainly due to be vindicated, for everyone was rushing incontinently into Hell-mouth without even the excuse of an Antichrist to mislead him. As matters stood now, Christ Himself would have to creep stealthily, hoping to be ignored, even into a cathedral to conduct a Mass, as in that panel of Hieronymus Bosch; the number of people who could not pronounce the Divine Name without a betraying stammer—or their own names, for that matter—had grown from a torrent to a deluge, and, ridiculously, hardly any of them were claiming any fraction of the possible profits in this world. They did not even know that they were on the winning side, or even that there was more than one side. No wonder that Ware had found so much fat in the cauldron, waiting to be skimmed.)

But as Ware had already warned Baines, not all of the spirits in the book were suitable for the experiment at hand. There were some, like MARCHOSIAS, who had hoped after an interval to be returned to the

Celestial choirs. In this hope, Ware was grimly certain, they were mistaken, and the only reward they would receive would be from the Emperor of the Pit, that kind of reward customarily given to fair-weather friends and summer soldiers. In the meantime, the evils they would be persuaded or compelled to do were minor and hardly worth the effort of invoking them. One, whom Ware had already mentioned to Baines, VASSAGO, was even said in the *Lesser Key* and elsewhere to be "good by nature"—not too trustworthy an ascription—and indeed was sometimes called upon by white magicians. Others in the hierarchy, like PHOENIX, controlled aspects of reality that were of little relevance to Baines' commission.

Taking up the pen of the Art, Ware made a list. When he was finished, he had written down forty-eight names. Considering the number of the Fallen, that was not a large muster; but he thought it would serve the purpose. He closed and locked the book, and after a pause to rebuke and torment the Guardian of his door, went out into the Easter morning to rehearse his Tanists.

No day, it seemed, had ever gone so slowly for Baines as this Easter, despite the diversion of the rehearsal; but at last it was night and over, and Ware pronounced himself ready to begin.

The Grand Circle now on the parquetry of the refectory bore a generic resemblance to the circle Ware had composed on Christmas Eve, but it was a great deal bigger, and much different in detail. The circle proper was made of strips of the skin of the sacrificial kid, with the hair still on it, fastened to the floor at the cardinal points with four nails that, Ware explained, had been drawn from the coffin of a child. On the northeast arc, under the word BERKAIAL, there rested on the strips the body of a male bat that had been drowned in blood; on the northeast, under the word AMASARAC, the skull of a parricide; on the southwest, under the word ASARADEL, the horns of a goat; and on the southwest, under the word ARIBECL, sat Ware's cat, to the secret of whose diet they were now all privy. (Indeed, there had not been much of moment to the rehearsal, and Baines had inferred that its chief object had been to impart to the rest of them such items of unpleasant knowledge as this.)

The triangle had been drawn inside the circle with a lump of haematite or lodestone. Under its base was drawn a figure consisting of a *chi* and a *rho* superimposed, resting on the line, with a cross to each side of it. Flanking the other two sides were the great candles of virgin wax, each stick sitting in the center of a crown of vervain. Three circles for the operators —Ware, Baines and Hess (Jack Ginsberg and Father Domenico would stand outside, in separate pentacles) —were inside the triangle, connected by a cross; the northern circle had horns drawn on it. At the pinnacle of the triangle sat a new brazier, loaded with newly consecrated charcoal. To the left side of the horned circle, which was to be Ware's, of course, was the lectern and the book of pacts, within easy reach.

At the rear of the room, before the curtained door to the kitchen, was another circle, quite as big as the first, in the center of which was a covered altar. That had been empty this afternoon; but there now lay upon it the nude body of the girl Ware had used to address as Gretchen. Her skin was paper-white except for its markings, and to Baines gave every apearance of being dead. A small twist of violet silk, nearly transparent and with some crumpled thing like a wad of tissue or a broken matzoh inside it, rested upon her navel. Her body appeared to have been extensively

written upon with red and yellow grease paint; some
of the characters might have been astrological, others
more like ideograms or cartouches. In default of knowing their meaning or even their provenance, they
simply made her look more naked.

The main door closed. Everyone was now in place.

Ware lit the candles, and then the fire in the brazier.
It was a task of Baines and Hess to feed the fire
periodically, as the time wore on, the one with brandy,
the other with camphor, taking care not to stumble
over their swords or leave their circles in the process.
As before, they had been enjoined to the strictest
silence, especially should any spirit speak to them
or threaten them.

Ware now reached out to the lectern and opened
his book. This time there were no preliminary ges-
tures, and no portents; he simply began to recite in a
gravid voice:

"I conjure and command thee, LUCIFUGE ROFOCALE,
by all the names wherewith thou mayst be constrained
and bound, SATAN, RANTAN, PALLANTRE, LUTIAS,
CORICACOEM, SCIRCIGREUR, *per sedem Baldarey et per
gratiam et diligentiam tuam habuisti ab eo hanc
nalatimanamilam,* as I command thee, *usor, dilapida-
tore, tenatore, seminatore, soignatore, devoratore, con-
citore, et seductore,* where are thou? Thou who im-
poseth hatred and propagateth enmities, I conjure
thee by Him who hath created thee for this ministry,
to fulfill my work! I cite thee, COLRIZIANA, OFFINA,
ALTA, NESTERA, FUARD, MENUET, LUCIFUGE ROFOCALE,
arise, arise, arise!"

There was no sound; but suddenly there was standing in the other circle a dim, steaming figure, perhaps
eight or nine feet tall. It was difficult to be sure what
it looked like, partly because some of the altar could
still be seen through it. To Baines it resembled a man

with a shaven head bearing three long, twisted horns, eyes like a spectral tarsier's, a gaping mouth, a pointed chin. It was wearing a sort of jerkin, coppery in color, with a tattered ruff and a fringed skirt; below the skirt protruded two bandy, hooved legs, and a fat, hairy tail, which twitched restlessly.

"What now?" this creature said in an astonishingly pleasant voice. The words, however were blurred. "I have not seen my son in many moons." Unexpectedly, it giggled, as though pleased by the pun.

"I adjure thee, speak more clearly," Ware said. "And what I wish, thou knowst full well."

"Nothing may be known until it is spoken." The voice seemed no less blurred to Baines, but Ware nodded.

"I desire then to release, as did the Babylonian from under the seal of the King of Israel, blessed be he, from Hellmouth into the mortal world all those demons of the False Monarchy whose names I shall subsequently call, and whose characters and signs I shall exhibit in my book, providing only that they harm not me and mine, and that they shall return whence they came at dawn, as it is always decreed."

"Providing no more than that?" the figure said. "No prescriptions? No desires? You were not always so easily satisfied."

"None," Ware said firmly. "They shall do as they will for this their period of freedom, except that they harm none here in my circles, and obey me when recalled, by rod and pact."

The demon glanced over its transparent shoulder. "I see that you have the appropriate fumigant to cense so many great lords, and my servants and satraps will have their several rewards in their deeds. So interesting a commission is new to me. Well. What have you for my hostage, to fulfill the forms?"

Ware reached into his vestments. Baines half expected to see produced another tear vase, but instead Ware brought out by a tail a live mouse, which he threw over the brazier as he had the vase, except not so far. The mouse ran directly toward the demon, circled it frantically three times outside the markings, and disappeared in the direction of the rear door, cheeping like a sparrow. Baines looked toward Ahktoi, but the cat did not even lick its chops.

"You are skilled and punctilious, my son. Call then when I have left, and I will send my ministers. Let nothing remain undone, and much will be done before the black cock crows."

"It is well. By and under this promise I discharge thee. OMGROMA, EPYN, SEYOK, SATANY, DEGONY, EPARYGON, GALLIGANON, ZOGOGEN, FERSTIGON, LUCIFUGE ROFOCALE, begone, begone, begone!"

"I shall see you at dawn." The prime minister of LUCIFER wavered like a flame, and, like a flame, went out.

Hess promptly cast camphor into the brazier. Recovering with a start from a near paralysis of fascination, Baines sprinkled brandy after it. The fire puffed. Without looking around, Ware brought out his lodestone, which he held in his left hand; with his right, he dipped the iron-headed point of his wand into the coals. Little licking points of blue light ran up it almost to his hand, as though the rod, too,, had been coated with brandy.

Holding the tonguing wand out before him like a dowsing rod, Ware strode ceremoniously out of the Grand Circle toward the altar. As he walked, the air around him began to grumble, as though a storm were gathering about his shaven head, but he paid the noise no attention. He marched on directly to the *locus spiritus,* and into it.

Silence fell at once. Ware said clearly:

"I, Theron Ware, master of masters, Karcist of Karcists, hereby undertake to open the book, and the seals thereof, which were forbidden to be broken until the breaking of the Seven Seals before the Seventh Throne. I have beheld SATAN as a bolt falling from heaven. I have crushed the dragons of the pit beneath my heel. I have commanded angels and devils. I undertake and command that all shall be accomplished as I bid, and that from beginning to end, alpha to omega, world without end, none shall harm us who abide here in this temple of the Art of Arts. *Aglan,* TETRAGRAM, *vaycheon stimulamaton ezphares retragrammaton olyaram irion esytion existion eryona onera orasym mozm messias soter* EMANUEL SABAOTH ADONAY, *te adoro, et te invoco.* Amen."

He took another step forward, and touched the flaming top of the rod to the veil of silk on the belly of the still girl. A little curl of blue-gray smoke began to arise from it, like ignited incense.

Ware now retreated, walking backward, toward the Grand Circle. As he did so, the fire on the wand died; but in the mortuary silence there now intruded a faint hissing, much like the first ignition of a squib. And there were indeed fireworks in inception. As Baines stared in gluttonous hypnosis, a small fountain of many-colored sparks began to rise from the fuse-like tissue on the abdomen of the body on the altar. More smoke poured forth. The air was becoming distinctly hazy.

The body itself seemed to be burning now, the skin peeling back like segments of an orange. Baines heard behind him an aborted retching noise in Jack Ginsberg's voice, but could not himself understand what the occasion for nausea could be. The body— whatever it had once been—now now only like a simu-

lacrum made of pith or papier-mâché, and charged
with some equivalent of Greek fire. Indeed, there was
already a strong taint of gunpowder overriding the
previous odors of incense and camphor. Baines rather
welcomed it—not that it was familiar, for it had been
centuries since black powder had been used in his
trade, but because he had begun to find the accumula-
tion of less business-like perfumes a little cloying.

Gradually, everything melted away into the smoke
except an underlay of architectural outline, against
which stood a few statues lit more along one side than
the other by one of the two sources of fire. Hess
coughed briefly; otherwise there was silence except
for the hissing of the pyre. Sparks continued to fly
upward, and sometimes, for an instant, they seemed to
form scribbled, incomprehensible words in the frame
of the unreal wall.

Ware's voice sounded remotely from one of the
statues:

"BAAL, great king and commander in the East, of
the Order of the Fly, obey me!"

Something began to form in the distance. Baines
had the clear impression that it was behind the altar,
behind the curtained door, indeed outside the palazzo
altogether, but he could see it nevertheless. It came
forward, growing, until he could also see that it was a
thing like a man, in a neat surcoat and snow-white
linen, but with two supernumerary heads, the one on
the left like a toad's, the other like a cat's. It swelled
soundlessly until at some moment it was inarguably
in the refectory; and then, still silently, had grown
past them and was gone.

"AGARES, duke in the East, of the Order of the Virtues, obey me!"

Again, a distant transparency, and silent. It came
on very slowly, manifesting like a comely old man

carrying a goshawk upon his wrist. Its slowness was necessitous, for it was riding astride an ambling crocodile. Its eyes were closed and its lips moved incessantly. Gradually, it too swelled past.

"GAMYGYN, marquis and president in Cartagra, obey me!"

This grew to be something like a small horse, or perhaps an ass, modest and unassuming. It dragged behind it ten naked men in chains.

"VALEFOR, powerful duke, obey me!"

A black-maned lion, again with three heads, the other two human, one wearing the cap of a hunter, the other the wary smile of a thief. It passed in a rush, without even a wind to mark its going.

"BARBATOS, great count and minister of SATANACHIA, obey me!"

But this was not one figure; it was four, like four crowned kings. With it and past it poured three companies of soldiers, their heads bowed and their expressions shuttered and still under steel caps. When all this troop had vanished, it was impossible to guess which among them had been the demon, or if the demon had ever appeared.

"PAIMON, great king, of the Order of the Dominions, obey me!"

Suddenly after all the hissing silence there was a blast of sound, and the room was full of capering things carrying contorted tubes and bladders, which might have been intended as musical instruments. The noise, however, resembled most closely a drove of pigs being driven down the chute of a slaughterhouse. Among the bawling, squealing dancers a crowned man rode upon a dromedary, bawling wordlessly in a great hoarse voice. The beast it rode on chewed grimly on some bitter cud, its eyes squeezed shut as if in pain.

"SYTRY!" Ware shouted. Instantly there was darkness and quiet, except for the hissing, which now had a faint overtone as of children's voices. *"Jussus secreta libenter detegit feminarum, eas ridens ludificansque ut se luxorise nudent,* great prince, obey me!"

This sweet and lissome thing was no less monstrous than the rest; it had a glowing human body, but was winged, and had the ridiculously small, smirking head of a leopard. At the same time, it was beautiful, in some way that made Baines feel both sick and eager at the same time. As it passed, Ware seemed to be pressing a ring against his lips.

"LERAJIE, powerful marquis, ELIGOR, ZEPAR, great dukes, obey me!"

As they were called together, so these three appeared together: the first an archer clad in green, with quiver and a nocked bow whose arrow dripped venom; the second, a knight with a scepter and a pennon-bearing lance; the third, an armed soldier clad in red. In contrast to their predecessor, there was nothing in the least monstrous about their appearance, nor any clues as to their spheres and offices, but Baines found them no less alarming for all that.

"AYPOROS, mighty earl and prince, obey me!"

Baines felt himself turning sick even before this creature appeared, and from the sounds around him, so did the others, even including Ware. There was no special reason for this apparent in its aspect, which was so grotesque as to have been comic under other circumstances: it had the body of an angel, with a lion's head, the webbed feet of a goose and the scut of a deer. "Transform, transform!" Ware cried, thrusting his wand into the brazier. The visitant promptly took on the total appearance of an angel, crown to toe, but the effect of the presence of something filthy and obscene remained.

"HABORYM, strong duke, obey me!"

This was another man-thing of the three-headed race—though the apparent relationship, Baines realized, must be pure accident—the human one bearing two stars on its forehead; the others were of a serpent and a cat. In its right hand it carried a blazing fire-brand, which it shook at them as it passed.

"NABERIUS, valiant marquis, obey me!"

At first it seemed to Baines that there had been no response to this call. Then he saw movement near the floor. A black cock with bleeding, empty eye sockets was fluttering around the outside of the Grand Circle. Ware menaced it with the wand, and it crowed hoarsely and was gone.

"GLASYALABOLAS, mighty president, obey me!"

This appeared to be simply a winged man until it smiled, when it could be seen to have the teeth of a dog. There were flecks of foam at the corners of its mouth. It passed soundlessly.

In the silence, Baines could hear Ware turning a page in his book of pacts, and remembered to cast more brandy into the brazier. The body on the altar had apparently long since been consumed; Baines could not remember how long it had been since he had seen the last of the word-forming sparks. The thick gray haze persisted, however.

"BUNE, thou strong duke, obey me!"

This apparition was the most marvelous yet, for it approached them borne on a galleon, which sank into the floor as it came nearer until they were able to look down through the floor onto its deck. Coiled there was a dragon with the familiar three heads, these being of dog, griffin and man. Shadowy figures, vaguely human, toiled around it. It continued to sink until it was behind them, and presumably thereafter.

Its passage left Baines aware that he was trembling

—not from fright, exactly, for he seemed to have passed beyond that, but from the very exhaustion of this and other emotions, and possibly also from the sheer weariness of having stood in one spot for so long. Inadvertently, he sighed.

"Silence," Ware said in a low voice. "And let nobody weaken or falter at this point. We are but half done with our calling—and of those remaining to be invoked, many are far more powerful than any we've yet seen. I warned you before, this Art takes physical strength as well as courage."

He turned another page. "ASTAROTH, grand treasurer, great and powerful duke, obey me!"

Even Baines had heard of this demon, though he could not remember where, and he watched it materialize with a stirring of curiosity. Yet it was nothing remarkable in the light of what he had seen already: an angelic figure, at once beautiful and foul, seated astride a dragon; it carried a viper in its right hand. He remembered belatedly that these spirits, never having been matter in the first place, had to borrow a body to make appearances like this, and would not necessarily pick the same one each time; the previous description of ASTAROTH that he had read, he now recalled, had been that of a piebald Negro woman riding on an ass. As the creature passed him, it smiled into his face, and the stench of its breath nearly knocked him down.

"ASMODAY, strong and powerful king, chief of the power of Amaymon, angel of chance, obey me!" As he called, Ware swept off his hat with his left hand, taking care, Baines noted, not to drop the lodestone as he did so.

This king also rode a dragon, and also had three heads—bull, man and ram. All three heads breathed fire. The creature's feet were webbed, as were its hands, in which it carried a lance and pennon; and it had a serpent's tail. Fearsome enough; but Baines was beginning to note a certain narrowness of invention among these infernal artisans. It also occurred to him to wonder, fortunately, whether this very repetitiveness was not deliberate, intended to tire him into inattentiveness, or lure him into the carelessness of contempt. *This thing might kill me if I even closed my eyes,* he reminded himself.

"FURFUR, great earl, obey me!"

This angel appeared as a hart and was past them in a single bound, its tail streaming fire like a comet.

"HALPAS, great earl, obey me!"

There was nothing to this apparition but a stock dove, also quickly gone. Ware was calling the names now as rapidly as he could manage to turn the pages, perhaps in recognition of the growing weariness of his Tanists, perhaps even of his own. The demons flashed by in nightmare parade: RAYM, earl of the Order of the Thrones, a man with a crow's head; SEPAR, a mermaid wearing a ducal crown; SABURAC, a lion-headed soldier upon a pale horse; BIFRONS, a great earl in the shape of a gigantic flea; ZAGAN, a griffin-winged bull; ANDRAS, a raven-headed angel with a bright sword, astride a black wolf; ANDREALPHUS, a peacock appearing amid the noise of many unseen birds; AMDUSCIAS, a unicorn among many musicians; DANTALIAN, a mighty duke in the form of a man but showing many faces both of men and women, with a book in his right hand; and at long last, that mighty king created next after LUCIFER and first to fall in battle before MICHAEL, formerly of the Order of the Virtues, BELIAL himself, beautiful and deadly in a chariot of fire as he had been worshiped in Babylon.

"Now, great spirits," Ware said, "because ye have diligently answered me and shown yourselves to my demands, I do hereby license ye to depart, without injury to any here. Depart, I say, yet be ye willing and ready to come at the appointed hour, when I shall duly exorcise and conjure you by your rites and seals. Until then, ye abide free. Amen."

He snuffed out the fire in the brazier with a closely fitting lid on which was graven the Third or Secret Seal of Solomon. The murk in the refectory began to lift.

"All right," Ware said in a matter-of-fact voice. Strangely, he seemed much less tired than he had after the conjuration of MARCHOSIAS. "It's over—or rather, it's begun. Mr. Ginsberg, you can safely leave your circle now, and turn on the lights."

When Ginsberg had done so, Ware also snuffed the candles. In the light of the shaded electrics the hall seemed in the throes of a cheerless dawn, although in fact the time was not much past midnight. There was nothing on the altar now but a small heap of fine gray ash.

"Do we really have to wait it out in here?" Baines said, feeling himself sagging. "I should think we'd be a lot more comfortable in your office—and in a better position to find out what's going on, too."

"We must remain here," Ware said firmly. "That, Mr. Baines, is why I asked you to bring in your transistor radio—to keep track of both the world and the time. For approximately the next eight hours, the area inside these immediate walls will be the only safe place on all the Earth."

XVI

Trappings, litter and all, the refectory now reminded Baines incongruously of an initiation room in a college fraternity house just after the last night of Hell Week. Hess was asleep on the long table that earlier had borne Ware's consecrated instruments. Jack Ginsberg lay on the floor near the main door, napping fitfully, mumbling and sweating. Theron Ware, after again warning everyone not to touch anything, had dusted off the altar and gone to sleep—apparently quite soundly—upon it, still robed and gowned.

Only Baines and Father Domenico remained awake. The monk, having prowled once around the margins of the room, had found an unsuspected low window behind a curtain, and now stood, with his back to them all, looking out at the black world, hands locked behind his back.

Baines sat on the floor with his own back propped against the wall next to the electric furnace, the transistor radio pressed to his ear. He was brutally uncomfortable, but he had found by experiment that this was the best place in the hall for radio reception—barring, of course, his actually entering one of the circles.

Even here, the reception was not very good. It wavered in and out maddeningly, even on powerful stations like Radio Luxembourg, and was liable to tear-ing blasts of static. These were usually followed, at intervals of a few seconds to several minutes, by bursts or rolls of thunder in the sky outside. Much of the time, too, as was usual, the clear spaces were occupied by nothing except music and commercials.

And thus far, what little news he had been able to pick up had been vaguely disappointing. There had been a major train wreck in Colorado; a freighter was foundering in a blizzard in the North Sea; in Guatemala, a small dam had burst, burying a town in an enormous mud slide; an earthquake was reported in Corinth—the usual budget of natural or near-natural disasters for any day.

In addition, the Chinese had detonated another hydrogen device; there had been another raiding incident on the Israeli-Jordanian border; black tribesmen had staged a rape and massacre on a government hospital in Rhodesia; the poor were marching on Washington again; the Soviet Union had announced that it would not be able to recover three dogs and a monkey it had put in orbit a week ago; the U.S. gained another bloody inch in Vietnam, and Premier Ky put his foot in it; and . . .

All perfectly ordinary, all going to prove what everyone of good sense already knew, that there was *no* safe place on the Earth either inside this room or without it, and probably never had been. What, Baines began to wonder, was the profit in turning loose so many demons, at so enormous an expenditure of time, effort and money, if the only result was to be just like reading any morning's newspaper? Of course, it might be that interesting private outrages were also being committed, but many newspaper and other publishers made fortunes on those in ordinary times, and in any event he could never hear of more than a fraction of them over this idiot machine.

Probably he would just have to wait until days or weeks later, when the full record and history of this night had been assembled and digested, when no doubt its full enormity might duly appear. He should have expected nothing else; after all, the full impact of a work of art is never visible in the sketches. All the same, he was obstinately disappointed to be deprived of the artist's excitement of watching the work growing on the canvas.

Was there anything that Ware could do about that? Almost surely not, or he would have done it already; it was clear that he had understood the motive behind the commission as well as he had understood its nature. Besides, it would be dangerous to wake him—he would need all his strength for the latter half of the experiment, when the demons began to return.

Resentfully, but with some resignation too, Baines realized that he himself had never been the artist here. He was only the patron, who could watch the colors being applied and the cartoon being filled, and could own the finished board or ceiling, but had never even in principle been capable of handling the brushes.

But there—what was that? The BBC was reporting:

"A third contingent of apparatus has been dispatched along the Thames to combat the Tate Gallery fire. Expert observers believe there is no hope of saving the gallery's great collection of Blake paintings, which include most of his illustrations for the *Inferno* and *Purgatorio* of Dante. Hope also appears to be lost for what amount to almost all the world's paintings by Turner, including his watercolors of the burning of the Houses of Parliament. The intense and sudden nature of the initial outbreak has lead to the suspicion that the fire is the work of an incendiary."

Baines sat up alertly, feeling an even more acute stab of hope, though all his joints protested painfully.

There was a crime with real style, a crime with symbolism, a crime with meaning. Excitedly, he remembered HARBORYM, the demon with the dripping firebrand. Now if there were to be more acts that imaginative . . .

The reception was getting steadily worse; it was extraordinarily tiring to be continuously straining to filter meaning out of it. Radio Luxembourg appeared to have gone off the air, or to have been shut out by some atmospheric disturbance. He tried Radio Milan, and got it just in time to hear it announce itself about to play all eleven of the symphonies of Gustav Mahler, one right after the other, an insane project for any station and particularly for an Italian one. Was that some demon's idea of a joke? Whatever the answer, it was going to take Radio Milan out of the newscasting business for well over twenty-four hours to come.

He cast further about the dial. There seemed to be an extraordinary number of broadcasts going out in languages he did not know or could even recognize, though he could get around passably in seventeen standard tongues and in any given year was fluent in a different set of three, depending on business requirements. It was almost as though someone had jammed an antenna on the crown of Babel.

Briefly, he caught a strong outburst of English; but it was only the Voice of America making piously pejorative sermonettes about the Chinese fusion explosion. Baines had known that that was coming for months now. Then the multilingual mumbling and chuntering resumed, interspersed occasionally with squeals of what might indifferently have been Pakistani jazz or Chinese opera.

Another segment of English shouted, " . . . with Cyanotabs! Yes, friends, one dose cures all ills! Guar-

anteed chockfull of crisp, crunchy atoms . . ." and
was replaced by a large boys' choir singing the
"Hallelujah Chorus," the words for which, however,
seemed to go, "Bison, bison! Rattus, rattus! Cardinalis!
Cardinalis!" Then more gabble, marvelously static-
free and sometimes hovering just on the edge of in-
telligibility.

The room stank abominably of an amazing mixture
of reeks: brandy, camphor, charcoal, vervain, gunpowder, flesh, sweat, perfume, incense, candle wicks,
musk, singed hair. Baines' head ached dully; it was
like trying to breathe inside the mouth of a vulture.
He longed to take a pull at the brandy bottle under
his rumpled alb, but he did not know how much of
what was left would be needed when Ware resumed
operations.

Across from him, something moved: Father Domenico had unlocked his hands and turned away from
the small window. He was now taking a few prim
steps toward Baines. The slight stir of human life
seemed to disturb Jack Ginsberg, who thrashed himself into an even more uncomfortable-looking position,
shouted hoarsely, and then began to snore. Father
Domenico shot a glance at him, and, stopping just
short of his side of the Grand Circle, beckoned.

"Me?" Baines said.

Father Domenico nodded patiently. Putting aside the
overheated little radio with less reluctance than he
would have imagined possible only an hour ago,
Baines heaved himself arthritically to his knees, and
then to his feet.

As he started to stumble toward the monk, something furry hurtled in front of him and nearly made
him fall: Ware's cat. It was darting toward the altar;
and in a soaring arc incredible in an animal of its
shameless obesity, leapt up there and settled down on

the rump of its sleeping master. It looked greenly at Baines and went itself to sleep, or appeared to.

Father Domenico beckoned again, and went back to the window. Baines limped after him, wishing that he had taken off his shoes; his feet felt as though they had turned into solid blocks of horn.

"What's the matter?" he whispered.

"Look out there, Mr. Baines."

Confused and aching, Baines peered past his un-invited and unimpressive Virgil. At first he could see nothing but the streaked steam on the inside of the glass, with a spume of fat snowflakes slurrying beyond it. Then he saw that the night was in fact not wholly dark. Somehow he could sense the undersides of turbulent clouds. Below, the window, like the one in Ware's office, looked down the side of the cliff and out over the sea, which was largely invisible in the snow whorls; so should the town have been, but it was in fact faintly luminous. Overhead, from frame to frame of the window, the clouds were overstitched with continuous streaks of dim fire, like phosphorescent contrails, long-lasting and taking no part in the weather.

"Well?" Baines said.

"You don't see anything?"

"I see the meteor tracks or whatever they are. And the light is odd—sheet lightning, I suppose, and maybe a fire somewhere in town."

"That's all?"

"That's all," Baines said, irritated. "What are you trying to do, panic me into waking Dr. Ware and calling it all quits? Nothing doing. We'll wait it out."

"All right," Father Domenico said, resuming his vigil. Baines stumped back to his corner and picked up the radio. It said:

". . . now established that the supposed Chinese

fusion test was actually a missile warhead explosion of at least thirty megatons, centered on Taiwan. Western capitals, already in an uproar because of the napalm murder of the U. S. President's widow in a jammed New York discotheque, are moving quickly to a full war footing and we expect a series of security blackouts on the news at any moment. Until that happens we will keep you informed of whatever important events come through. We pause for station identification. Owoo. Eeg. Oh, piggly baby, I caught you—cheatin' on me—owoo . . ."

Baines twisted the dial savagely, but the howling only became more bestial. Down the wall to his right, Hess twisted his long body on the table and suddenly sat upright, swinging his stockinged feet to the floor.

"Jesus Christ," he said huskily. "Did I hear what I thought I heard?"

"Dead right you did," Baines said quietly, and not without joy; but he, too, was worried. "Slide over here and sit down. Something's coming to a head, and it's nothing like we'd expected—or Ware either."

"Hadn't we better call a halt, then?"

"No. Sit down, goddamn it. I don't think we *can* call a halt—and even if we could, I don't want to give our clerical friend over there the satisfaction."

"You'd rather have World War Three?" Hess said, sitting down obediently.

"I don't know that that's what's going to happen. We contracted for this. Let's give it the benefit of the doubt. Either Ware's in control, or he should be. Let's wait and see."

"All right," Hess said. He began to knead his fingers together. Baines tried the radio once more, but nothing was coming through except a mixture of *The Messiah*, Mahler and The Supremes.

Jack Ginsberg whined in his pseudo-sleep. After a while, Hess said neutrally:

"Baines?"

"What is it?"

"What kind of a thing do you think this is?"

"Well, it's either World War Three or it isn't. How can I know yet?"

"I didn't ask you that . . . not what you think it *is*. I asked you, what *kind* of a thing do you think it is? You ought to have some sort of notion. After all, you contracted for it."

"Oh. Hmm. Father Domenico said it might turn out to be Armageddon. Ware didn't think so, but he hasn't turned out to be very right up to now. I can't guess, myself. I haven't been thinking in these terms very long."

"Nor have I," Hess said, watching his fingers weave themselves in and out. "I'm still trying to make sense of it in the old terms, the ones that used to make sense of the universe to me. It isn't easy. But you'll remember I told you I was interested in the history of science. That involves trying to understand why there wasn't any science for so long, and why it went into eclipse almost every time it was rediscovered. I think I know why now. I think the human mind goes through a sort of cycle of fear. It can only take so much accumulated knowledge, and then it panics, and starts inventing reasons to throw everything over and go back to a Dark Age . . . every time with a new, invented mystical reason."

"You're not making very much sense," Baines said. He was still also trying to listen to the radio.

"I didn't expect you to think so. But it happens. It happens about every thousand years. People start out happy with their gods, even though they're frightened of them. Then, increasingly, the world becomes secularized, and the gods seem less and less relevant. The temples are deserted. People feel guilty about that, but not much. Then, suddenly, they've had all the secularization they can take, they throw their wooden shoes into the machines, they take to worshiping Satan or the Great Mother, they go into a Hellenistic period or take up Christianity, *in hoc signo vinces*— I've got those all out of order but it happens, Baines, it happens like clockwork, every thousand years. The last time was the chiliastic panics just before the year A.D. 1000, when everyone expected the Second Coming of Christ and realized that they didn't dare face up to Him. *That* was the heart, the center, the whole reason of the Dark Ages. Well, we've got another millennium coming to a close now, and people are terrified of *our* secularization, our nuclear and biological weapons, our computers, our overprotective medicine, everything, and they're turning back to the worship of unreason. Just as you've done—and I've helped you. Some people these days worship flying saucers because they don't dare face up to Christ. You've turned to black magic. Where's the difference?"

"I'll tell you where," Baines said. "Nobody in the whole of time has ever seen a saucer, and the reasons for believing that anybody has are utterly pitiable. Probably they can be explained just as you've explained them, and never mind about Jung and his thump-headed crowd. But, Adolph, you and I *have* seen a demon."

"Do you think so? I don't deny it. I think it very possible. But Baines, are you sure? How do you *know* what you think you know? We're on the eve of World War Three, which we engineered. Couldn't all this be a hallucination we conjured up to remove some of our guilt? Or is it possible that it isn't happening at all, and that we're as much victims of a chiliastic panic as more formally religious people are? That makes more sense to me than all this medieval mumbo-jumbo about demons. I don't mean to deny the evidence of my sense, Baines. I only mean to ask you, what is it worth?"

"I'll tell you what I know," Baines said equably, "though I can't tell you how I know it and I won't bother to try. First, something is happening, and that something is real. Second, you and I and Ware and everyone else who wanted to make it happen, therefore *did* make it happen. Third, we're turning out to be wrong about the outcome—but no matter what it is, it's *our* outcome. We contracted for it. Demons, saucers, fallout—what's the difference? Those are just signs in the equation, parameters we can fill any way that makes the most intermediate sense to us. Are you happier with electrons than with demons? Okay, good for you. But what I like, Adolph, what *I* like is the result. I don't give a damn about the means. I invented it, I called it into being, I'm paying for it—and no matter how else you describe it, *I made it, and it's mine*. Is that clear? *It's mine.* Every other possible fact about it, no matter what that fact might turn out to be, is a stupid footling technicality that I hire people like you and Ware not to bother me with."

"It seems to me," Hess said in a leaden monotone, "that we are all insane."

At that same moment, the small window burst into an intense white glare, turning Father Domenico into the most intense of inky silhouettes.

"You may be right," Baines said. "There goes Rome."

Father Domenico, his eyes streaming, turned away from the dimming frame and picked his way slowly to the altar. After a long moment of distaste, he took

Theron Ware by the shoulder and shook him. The cat hissed and jumped sidewise.

"Wake up, Theron Ware," Father Domenico said formally. "I charge you, awake. Your experiment may now wholly and contractually be said to have gone astray, and the Covenant therefore satisfied. Ware! Ware! Wake up, damn you!"

XVII

Baines looked at his watch. It was 3:00 A.M.

Ware awoke instantly, swung to his feet with a spring and without a word started for the window. At the same instant, the agony that had been Rome swept over the building. The shock wave had been attenuated by distance and the jolt was not heavy, but the window Father Domenico had uncurtained sprang inward in a spray of flying glass needles. More glass fell out from behind the drapes which hung below the ceiling, like an orchestra of celestas.

As far as Baines could see, nobody was more than slightly cut. Not that a serious wound could have made any difference now, with the Last Death already riding on the winds.

Ware was not visibly shaken. He simply nodded once and wheeled toward the Grand Circle, stooping to pick up his dented paper hat. No, he was moved—his lips were pinched white. He beckoned to them all.

Baines took a step toward Jack Ginsberg, to kick him awake if necessary. But the special executive assistant was already on his feet, trembling and wild-eyed. He seemed, however, totally unaware of where he was: Baines had to push him bodily into his minor circle.

"And stay there," Baines added, in a voice that should have been able to scar diamonds. But Jack gave no sign of having heard it.

Baines went hastily to his Tanist's place, checking for the bottle of brandy. Everyone else was already in position, even the cat, which in fact had vaulted to its post promptly upon having been dumped off Ware's rear.

The sorcerer lit the brazier, and began to address the dead air. He was hardly more than a sentence into this invocation before Baines realized for the first time, in his freezing heart, that this was indeed the last effort—and that indeed they might all still be saved.

Ware was making his renunciation, in his own black and twisted way—the only way his fatally proud soul could ever be brought to make it. He said:

"I invoke and conjure thee, LUCIFUGE ROFOCALE, and fortified with the Power and the Supreme Majesty, I strongly command thee by BARALEMENSIS, BALDA-CHIENSIS, PAUMACHIE, APOLORESEDES and the most potent princes GENIO, LIACHIDE, ministers of the Tartarean seat, chief princes of the seat of APOLOGIA in the ninth region, I exorcise and command thee, LUCI-FUGE ROFOCALE, by Him who spake and it was done, by the Most Holy and glorious Names ADONAI, EL, ELOHIM, ELOHE, ZEBAOTH, ELION, ESCHERCE, JAH, TETRAGRAMMATON, SADAI, do thou and thine forthwith appear and show thyself unto me, regardless of how thou art previously charged, from whatever part of the world, without tarrying!

"I conjure thee by Him to Whom all creatures are obedient, by this ineffable Name, TETRAGRAMMATON JEHOVAH, by which the elements are overthrown, the air is shaken, the sea turns back, the fire is generated, the earth moves and all the hosts of things celestial, of things terrestrial, of things infernal, do tremble and are confounded together, come. ADONAI, King of kings, commands thee!"

There was no answer, except an exterior grumble of thunder.

"Now I invoke, conjure and command thee, LUCIFUGE ROFOCALE, to appear and show thyself before this circle, by the Name of ON ... by the Name Y and V, which Adam heard and spake ... by the Name of JOTH, which Jacob learned from the angel on the night of his wrestling and was delivered from the hands of his brother ... by the Name of AGLA, which Lot heard and was saved with his family ... by the Name ANEHEXETON, which Aaron spake and was made wise ... by the Name SCHEMES AMATHIA, which Joshua invoked and the Sun stayed upon his course ... by the Name EMMANUEL, by which the three children were delivered from the fiery furnace ... by the Name ALPHA-OMEGA, which Daniel uttered, and destroyed Bel and the dragon ... by the Name ZEBAOTH, which Moses named, and all the rivers and the waters in the land of Egypt were turned into blood ... by the Name HAGIOS, by the Seal of ADONAI, by those others, which are JETROS, ATHENOROS, PARACLETUS ... by the dreadful Day of Judgment ..., by the changing sea of glass which is before the face of the Divine Majesty ... by the four beasts before the Throne ... by all these Holy and most potent words, come thou, and come thou quickly. Come, come! ADONAI, King of kings, commands thee!"

Now, at last, there was a sound: a sound of laughter. It was the laughter of Something incapable of joy, laughing only because It was compelled by Its nature to terrify. As the laughter grew, that Something formed.

It was not standing in the Lesser Circle or appearing from the Gateway, but instead was sitting on the altar, swinging Its cloven feet negligently. It had a goat's head, with immense horns, a crown that flamed

like a torch, level human eyes, and a Star of David on
Its forehead. Its haunches, too, were caprine. Between,
the body was human, though hairy and with drag-
ging black pinions like a crow's growing from Its
shoulder blades. It had women's breasts and an
enormous erection, which it nursed alternately with
hands folded into the gesture of benediction. On one
shaggy forearm was tattooed *Solve;* on the other,
Coagula.

Ware fell slowly to one knee.

"*Adoramus te,* PUT SATANACHIA," he said, laying
his wand on the ground before him. "And again . . .
ave, ave."

AVE, BUT WHY DO YOU HAIL ME? the monster said in
a petulant bass voice, at once deep and mannered, like
a homosexual actor's. IT WAS NOT I YOU CALLED.

"No, Baphomet, master and guest. Never for an
instant. It is everywhere said that you can never be
called, and would never appear."

YOU CALLED ON THE GOD, WHO DOTH NOT APPEAR. I
AM NOT MOCKED.

Ware bowed his head lower. "I was wrong."

AH! BUT THERE IS A FIRST TIME FOR EVERYTHING. YOU
MIGHT HAVE SEEN THE GOD AFTER ALL. BUT NOW INSTEAD
YOU HAVE SEEN ME. AND THERE IS ALSO A LAST TIME
FOR EVERYTHING. I OWE YOU A MOMENT OF THANKS.
WORM THOUGH YOU ARE, YOU ARE THE AGENT OF ARMA-
GEDDON. LET THAT BE WRITTEN, BEFORE ALL WRITINGS,
LIKE ALL ELSE, GO INTO THE EVERLASTING FIRE.

"No!" Ware cried out. "Oh living God, no! This
cannot be the Time! You break the Law! Where is
the AntiChrist—"

WE WILL DO WITHOUT THE ANTICHRIST. HE WAS
NEVER NECESSARY. MEN HAVE ALWAYS LED THEMSELVES
UNTO ME.

"But—master and guest—the Law—"

WE SHALL ALSO DO WITHOUT THE LAW. HAVE YOU NOT HEARD? THOSE TABLETS HAVE BEEN BROKEN.

There was a hiss of indrawn breath from both Ware and Father Domenico; but if Ware had intended some further argument, he was forestalled. To Baines' right, Dr. Hess said in a voice of high ultraviolet hysteria:

"I don't see you, Goat."

"Shut up!" Ware shouted, almost turning away from the vision.

"I don't see you," Hess said doggedly. "You're nothing but a silly zoological mixture. A mushroom dream. You're not real. Goat. Go away. Poof!"

Ware turned in his Karcist's circle and lifted his magician's sword against Hess in both hands; but, at the last minute, he seemed to be afraid to step out against the wobbling figure of the scientist.

HOW GRACIOUS OF YOU TO SPEAK TO ME, AGAINST THE RULES. WE UNDERSTAND, YOU AND I, THAT RULES WERE MADE TO BE BROKEN. BUT YOUR FORM OF ADDRESS DOES NOT QUITE PLEASE ME. LET US PROLONG THE CONVERSATION, AND I WILL EDUCATE YOU. ETERNALLY, FOR A BEGINNING.

Hess did not answer. Instead he howled like a wolf and charged blindly out of the Grand Circle, his head down, toward the altar. The Sabbath Goat opened Its great mouth and gulped him down like a fly.

THANK YOU FOR THE SACRIFICE, It said thickly. Anyone ELSE? THEN IT IS TIME I LEFT.

"Stand to, stupid and disobedient!" Father Domenico's voice rang out from Baines' right side. A cloth fluttered out of the monk's circle onto the floor. "Behold thy confusion, if thou be disobedient! Behold the Pentacle of Solomon which I have brought into thy presence!"

FUNNY LITTLE MONK, I WAS NEVER IN THAT BOTTLE!

"Hush and be still, fallen star. Behold in me the person of the Exorcist, who is called OCTINIMOES, in the midst of delusion armed by the Lord God and fearless. I am thy master, in the name of the Lord BATHAL, rushing upon ABRAC, ABEOR, coming upon BEROR!"

The Sabbath Goat looked down upon Father Domenico almost kindly. His face red, Father Domenico reached into his robes and brought out a crucifix, which he thrust toward the altar like a sword.

"Back to Hell, devil! In the name of Christ our Lord!"

The ivory cross exploded like a Prince Rupert's Drop, strewing Father Domenico's robe with dust. He looked down at his horribly empty hands.

TOO LATE, MAGICIAN. EVEN THE BEST EFFORTS OF YOUR WHITE COLLEGE ALSO HAVE FAILED—AND AS THE HEAVENLY HOSTS ALSO WILL FAIL. WE ARE ABROAD AND ALOOSE, AND WILL NOT BE PUT BACK.

The great head bent to look down upon Theron Ware.

AND YOU ARE MY DEARLY BELOVED SON, IN WHOM I AM WELL PLEASED. I GO TO JOIN MY BROTHERS AND LOVERS IN THE REST OF YOUR WORK. BUT I SHALL BE BACK FOR YOU. I SHALL BE BACK FOR YOU ALL. THE WAR IS ALREADY OVER.

"Impossible!" Father Domenico cried, though choking with the dust of the exploded crucifix. "It is written that in that war you will at last be conquered and chained!"

OF COURSE, BUT WHAT DOES THAT PROVE? EACH OF THE OPPOSING SIDES IN ANY WAR ALWAYS PREDICTS VICTORY. THEY CANNOT BOTH BE RIGHT. IT IS THE FINAL BATTLE THAT COUNTS, NOT THE PROPAGANDA. YOU MADE A MISTAKE—AND AH, HOW YOU WILL PAY!

"One moment . . . please," Father Domenico said.

"If you would be so kind . . . I see that we have failed. . . . Would you tell us, *where* did we fail?"

The Goat laughed, spoke three words, and vanished.

The dawn grew, red, streaked, dull, endless. From Ware's window the sleeping town slumped down in rivers of cold lava toward the sea—but there was no sea; as Father Domenico had seen hours ago, the sea had withdrawn, and would not be back again except as a tsunami after the Corinth earthquake. Circles of desolation spread away from the ritual circles. Inside them, the last magicians waited for the now Greatest Powers to come back for them.

It would not be long now. In all their minds and hearts echoed those last three words. World without end. End without world.

God is dead.